ODDS AND ENDS

Stories and Essays From the Sixties

By

Paul David Robinson

Cover design by Katrina Joyner

Copyright 1959-69, 2018

Kindle Direct Publishing Edition

ODDS AND ENDS

Stories and Essays From the Sixties

By

Paul David Robinson

Cover design by Katrina Joyner

Copyright 1959-69, 2018

Kindle Direct Publishing Edition

ISBN-13: 978-1-944675-14-1

ISBN-10: 1-944675-14-0

ODDS AND ENDS
Stories and Essays From the Sixties

TABLE OF CONTENTS

ODDS AND ENDS
Stories and Essays From the Sixties

TABLE OF CONTENTS
Continued

MECHANICAL MAN:
FROM UTILITY TO SCRAP

John Maynard Kingsley moaned as he rolled over in the double bed. His arm bumped the woman's stomach and the soft of the impact awoke him. He opened his eyes to find himself lying on his back in the middle of the bed. His eyes stared up at the globular light fixture. With layers of dust disguising its original yellow color, the fixture appeared a sickening green in the early morning light.

Kingsley felt a warm hand slip beneath his pajama top and creep up his stomach to the top of his chest. There her fingertips tickled the curled hairs. Keeping her arm where it was upon his chest, Kingsley's wife unbuttoned his pajama top and unsnapped the waistband of his pajama bottom. (Kingsley had mixed his two pairs of pajamas again.) The woman nuzzled his throat until he rolled over to meet her.

After his wife had gone to the kitchen in her nightgown to prepare breakfast, Kingsley lay back in the middle of the bed with his head between the two pillows; he stared up at the light fixture. His wife called to him from the kitchen to tell him that breakfast would be ready in fifteen minutes and that he should wake the children.

Kingsley wiggled to the right side of the bed, turned on the fulcrum of his buttocks, and placed both feet on the floor. He went to the closet, stripped off his sweaty pajamas and pulled on his bathrobe. He walked down the hall to the children's rooms, awoke the two elder children and told them both to be out of bed in five minutes. Kingsley walked back down the hall and into the bathroom. He flipped on the ceiling light, pulled off his robe and hung it on the clothes-hook on the back of the door.

Kingsley stepped up to the toilet and urinated into its unflushed contents. "That woman!" he said to himself. He shrugged the thought away and flushed the toilet. He stepped into the bathtub and drew the shower curtain all the way around. As he showered, soaped, and showered again, Kingsley heard three flushes of the toilet that informed him that probably all three children were up.

When Kingsley drew the shower curtain aside, he saw his three-year-old daughter trying to put toothpaste on her miniature toothbrush.

[ORIGINAL ENDING]

(He stepped out of the tub to help her, but slipped on some water slopped onto the floor. He fell backwards into the tub, his head slamming against the faucet. His skull split. Kingsley died instantaneously.)[1]

[ALTERNATE ENDING]

He stepped out of the bathtub, reached for the towel hanging on the towel rod beside the door, and dried himself. He hung the towel around his neck and then helped his daughter

---

[1] This is the original end to this story which was submitted for credit on March 27, 1965. I was thinking about my father when I wrote this. My father's favorite quote was: "Tomorrow and tomorrow and tomorrow creeps on in that petty pace from day to day to the last syllable of recorded time." I always thought that he felt that he was just going through the motions of life and not really living. That may have been why he had so many affairs: trying to spice up his boring life with something that felt good. The alternate ending doesn't fit the Mechanical Man title. That was why I left it off of the original story.

loosen the cap of the toothpaste tube.

He admonished her for carelessness when she squeezed out too much and it spilled all over her hand and onto the floor. She had missed the head of the brush completely. Kingsley cleaned up the mess on the floor and washed the child's hand at the sink before he guided her in squeezing out the toothpaste and then in the brushing of her tiny teeth. He helped her climb the stepstool and spit into the sink; then he used his hand to give her a swallow of water from the faucet to rinse her mouth and spit.

She looked up at him and smiled. He looked down at her and gave her a kiss on the mouth. He helped her get down from the stepstool and she left the bathroom.

He could taste the toothpaste from her mouth on his lips as he filled the sink half full of hot water. He moistened and lathered his face; then he shaved with his safety razor. He brushed his teeth before wiping away the remaining lather on his face with a washcloth and then drying his face with the towel hanging around his neck.

He tossed the towel into the clothes hamper and then he applied aftershave lotion and deodorant. He slipped back into his bathrobe and headed for the bedroom to get dressed.

He hung the bathrobe on the clothes hook on the back of the closet door and went to his chest of drawers and got into jockey shorts and an undershirt. He went back to the closet for a pair of dress pants and a dress shirt. After he put on his belt, he sat down on the bed and got into socks and shoes. Then he combed his hair and went into the kitchen for breakfast.

After breakfast, he made sure that the children had their homework ready for school. Then he went into his office and put the papers that he brought from work into his attaché case.

When he walked into the bedroom to get his suit coat, his wife was pulling on her panties. With an impish grin he shoved his right hand between her legs before she could get her panties up. He put his left arm around her back and kissed her as he gave her an orgasm with his finger.

He let her stand upright as he got his suit coat out of the closet. He slipped into it and headed back to the hall closet for his overcoat. His wife was dressed by then and followed him into the living room. She held his overcoat for him as he got into it. He turned around and kissed her again for a long time. He loved to kiss her before she put on her makeup. Her lips wouldn't leave a sign of lipstick on his face to embarrass him at work.

He whispered, "After you take the kids to school, don't forget to take the station wagon to the service station for that oil change."

She nodded her head.

He kissed her again for a longer time. Then he got his attaché case and went into the garage and got into his commuter car, a two-door Volkswagen bug.

He allowed the bug to warm up for a moment. Then he backed out of the garage. He waved to his wife as she closed the garage door. She waved back. Then he was out on the street and headed out of the subdivision.

As he drove, whenever he had the opportunity, he would smell the finger he had used to diddle his wife. He could smell that wonderful aroma on it. He had to reach down and adjust his erection so that he could drive more comfortably. He was looking forward to getting into bed with her that night.

He took the cloverleaf up to the expressway. As he was about to merge with traffic, a fast moving semi in the slow lane struck his VW bug and hurtled it over the guardrail and thirty feet into the air. It landed bottom up on the grass in the middle of the cloverleaf below. The roof of the VW was crushed flat.

Kingsley died instantaneously.[2]

---

[2] I found this second ending in my notes. What do you think? Do you prefer the original ending that I submitted or this alternate ending that I found in my notes?

NIGHT CALL

Jenson rolled over in his bed, taking his pillow with him. He pulled the ends of the pillow down to cover his ears. He could only hear a faint buzzing sound that way. He closed his eyes.

Yes, Jenson could go back to sleep and ignore the telephone, but he opened his eyes again and reached out for the handset. He knew it was probably some kind of emergency.

"Hello?" Jenson said quizzically into the mouthpiece, "Repeat please. . . . Yes, Michael, I can hear you. . . . No, it's just that you are talking much too fast and much too loud. . . I didn't mean for you to take it that way. Your voice didn't hurt my eardrum; your excitement startled me. . . That is perfectly alright. – We are still friends. . . . No, you didn't wake her up. She is staying with her mother this fortnight. . . . No, not a fight. Only it's been two years now since she last saw her mother. And how are your children? . . . . That is wonderful! Phyllis is planning to have a boy next year. . . I don't know why she wants a boy. She keeps telling me that I must have been cute once-upon-a-time. . . . Yes. You've heard about our arguments then. . . . No, that wasn't it at all. She wasn't throwing the vase at me. She was throwing it at my sculpture, only I was close enough to step in the way. . . . Yes. She has always loathed it. . . Oh, no, not at all. She's just that way. Why else would she want a baby boy? . . . She wants to find out how cute I must have been once-upon-a-time. . . . Yes? . . . . You must be kidding! . . . That is really hard to believe. . . . You mean to say he actually did drain their swimming pool by dynamiting a hole in the bottom of it? . . . I knew he was mad at them, but I never thought he would carry out his threat. I hope he offered to pay for the repair. . . . I knew he would. He's a sweet guy. By the way, you called me about something? . . . Oh, yes. I do recall you telling me that earlier this week. Washing lye through the pipes didn't clean it out? . . . I see. I'll be there as soon as I can. . . Yes. . . . All right. . . I'll see you in a few minutes." Jenson hung up the telephone.

He sat up and stretched before swinging his legs over the side of the bed.

"A blocked sewer," he muttered to himself as he stripped off his pajamas.[3]

---

[3] Why did I write this? I don't' know. Maybe it was a part of something else that I had already written. It was in my file entitled: Ideas for short stories.

PARIDISE LOST

Once upon a time there lived beside a sea shore, very intelligent creatures called Linques. They were hardy mammals and practiced evolution whole-heartedly. In time, the science of Philosophy was developed and all Linques became practical philosophers. One of the more brilliant Linques discovered, in his spare time, Truth and was so distraught by its consequences that he died without leaving a single disciple.

This brilliant Linque's untimely death was a mystery to all of his acquaintances. All of these Linques pondered though none could conceive an answer. Finally, these Linques delegated one of the more plodding of their numbers (who wasn't good for much else anyway) to solve the mystery.

The poor Linque spent two generations to discover Truth again. When he attempted to reveal Truth to others, no one would believe him. The plodding Linque was forced to show them naked Truth.

Once most Linques felt the nail holes of Truth, they believed. However, there were a few pig-headed Linques who even felt the spear-wound of Truth and could still call it hogwash.

Most of the Linques recoiled at the thought of Truth and refused to accept it. They just would not believe that Truth was the non-existence of any kind of god and of all sorts of purposes, and that the brilliant Linque had died of a broken heart.

As is evidenced by all following history, the result of this occurrence was dissension and anguish. Leaders arose for each side, proclaiming truth and Truth. Naturally, Truth lost the campaign for followers.

The greater proportion of the Linques who confronted Truth accepted it, but most Linques were happier in ignorance (they claimed) and refused to confront Truth as they practiced evolution wholeheartedly. Commonly enough, the Linques following Truth were persecuted and discriminated against by the majority of ignorants.

Then the time came that Missing, the greatest Linque thinker, became the leader of the minority. Missing developed for his followers a new philosophy: Since Life held no actual purpose and there was no god, why evolve and build civilizations; why not stop fooling oneself with delusionary tactics; why fret about tomorrow, just enjoy what moments of life one has.

The end result of Missing's new Philosophy was that he and his followers remained behind on the sea shore when the disillusioned majority marched into the interior to evolve and build civilizations. Missing's group of Linques (now immortalized as the Missing Linques) frolicked in the water as their ignorant and pig-headed counterparts evolved and built civilizations.

The Missing Linques became more expert in the art of swimming, more at home in the water. Since the Missing Linques were highly intelligent, they had no need of much time for feeding. They would spend most of their time frolicking in the water or sunning themselves as they floated or swam lazily at the water's surface. The Missing Linques met all dangers as they occurred, and lived exemplary existential existences.

The Missing Linques did not evolve to build frivolities of no purpose, such as civilizations. They evolved with the intention of attaining the form best suited for frolicking. They did this by choice, on porpoise, and thanks to Lewis Carroll.[4]

---

[4] I wrote this in high school in 1960.

MANIA

While strolling through the park
    One day
In the merry, merry month of
    May,
I was taken by surprise
By a pair of blood-shot eyes.[5]

It may seem a wee bit funny, but it isn't. It wasn't a merry month, but the hottest, most despicable in three thousand years. The park was a jungle of trees, swamps, and snakes. To go for a stroll in that abominable mess would take a lot of gall, even a hint of insanity. You would stroll down an avenue two feet wide, walled on each side by a nearly impenetrable barrier of trees, underbrush, and bogs.

I must have been crazy to go out of my cave! I must have been possessed by the devil! Why didn't I heed the warnings? I saw the heat and moisture

---

[5] The original song was published by Ed Haley in 1884. In 1961, our high school English class was supposed to write a theme. The tune and the words just came to me at that moment and I borrowed it and altered it a little for this story.

rise from the jungle; I saw the bluish tinge on the bark! Why? Why?

My father had told me that one day this would happen. Yes, and his father had told him; his father's father had told his father; and so on for fifty generations! But I – I – a foolhardy simpleton – pushed aside the fears that had been building up for generations, and went for a stroll.

I stood straight and tall, unflinching! – And walked into the park. I paid no heed to the greater rustling among the leaves. I showed no fear when I saw with my mind's eye the creature watching me. I knew I was being followed and sensed the increased anxiety of my unconscious. But I walked on, past a huge bog and into the interior of the park.

It became darker; the sun was setting. For the first time, I felt fear. I wanted to turn back, but I was being followed and would fall prey to the creature by walking right into him. I went on feeling my adversary creeping closer in his preparations to pounce on me, its victim. I was terrified! I began to run. I ran; I ran; I ran! Hysteria was mounting within me. I screamed and ran faster. I ran with the strength of a maniac.

Night came and with it even greater fears! I feared stepping off the trail into a bog and strangling in the dirty, stinking muck as the thing watched me and laughed, like the fiend it is, as I died. I feared tripping over a root and falling prey to the quick devil as he took advantage of my misfortune. I hated and feared most that I would get lost and run into that thing and find my hands against his slimy loathsome flesh. Just thinking of touching the creature made me shudder and break my stride.

I ran on through the night, thanking all I felt holy that the moon was out and shone its light on my trail. I ran the hours and my hopes away as day approached, knowing that I could not keep up my pace much longer.

I tripped and lost my balance. To keep from falling, I had to slow down. It took much longer than expected to get my pace back up to where it was. I was tired, but found my pace and forced myself on.

The first light filtered through the trees and my hopes brightened as did my surroundings. The sun came out completely and I saw ahead the edge of the jungle. I was soon to be free of that hideous park! Happiness filled my soul and I increased my speed, running faster and faster!

The sun shone brightly on a meadow ahead. Beyond the meadow, a little rise separated the jungle from a vast plain. That plain, free from trees, bogs – all dangers – was sanctuary.

I ran across the meadow to the top of the little hill. There I stopped and turned to look at the jungle that I had just left. I laughed at the dangers behind me and screamed defiance to the creature that had once filled my heart with terror.

I looked toward the plain with my head held high: I had walked where no other had dared to walk and I had come out unaccosted, free!

Then I looked more directly in front of me. I saw there a small tree and a few large rocks. I smiled at this last reminder of the jungle. I turned away from it, but out of the corner of my eye, I saw movement.

I faced the tree. My smile faded! All the color left my face a deathly white! I stared in horror into two blood-shot eyes. I saw a fiendish grin on the countenance of my accoster. I was stupefied! I stood motionless, not even breathing.

The thing spoke: "Hello, fella!" it said with all the cynicism it could muster. I didn't move but stared transfixed into those beady eyes.

The thing stretched itself out to me and touched me! I screamed a voiceless cry of anguish and horror and fell forward on my face.

When I awoke, I was a new creature. I was me, yet something else too. I understood, now, and felt the terror of symbiosis![6]

---

[6] I wrote this in 1961 for sophomore high school English.

THE VANISHING PENCILS[7]

Around the school lately there have been a large number of pencils being missed. It almost seems as if the Irish Little People or the gnomes have been taking our pencils and leaving them to the terrible fate of being lost. Since that is not the cause of our pencils being "vanished", we must accept the fact that there is among us a group (Shall we call them gnomes?) that is on a wild pencil spree at our expense. This group of gnomes is using pencils at a very fast rate, but of course they would not think of bringing or using their own. To help the situation, I would suggest that all of us bring extra pencils to loan this pencil-shy group of gnomes. Maybe, if we loan our extra to them, our gnomes will make an effort to return them.

---

[7] This was written in the spring of 1959.

WRITING A THEME

When writing a theme mistakes are often made. The most ordinary mistakes are usually among the following: paragraphs on punctuation, spelling, and the use of words.[8]

Punctuation is a nuisance while writing themes. The comma is the ordinariest. And when the teacher is grading a theme after classes; it is most missed. There are many others that are rong also. So, be careful.

When spelling a word usully forget to put in the korect letters, even though stupidity is the most involved. The letters "i" and "e" are the displaciest of all; especially when riting a theme.

Even so I believe, that finding the rite words to go into the write places is the uses of words; like in the sentence: "the fishes were rapped in a sheet of papper and cent to the house 'cross the street".

---

[8] The mistakes in this theme are intentional.

The theme is usually rightten with care but mistakes offen happen. So! I wished to wish you all good luck on ritting yer nex theme.[9]

MEMORANDUM

"How in the world have I gotten myself into such a predicament?" I thought. However under the, not gentle, strokes of my backscratcher (I do believe he is trying to skin me.), I soon began to collect all the data concerning some previous events.

I had been meandering along in my usual carefree manner. Then I saw it! I exploded, "Get that cotton pickin' thing out of my way! I ain't gonna fall for that line again."

I remembered the first time that I was beguiled by this line. I had never felt this way before in all my young life; I was entranced; my desire for it was so tremendous and overwhelming, that I took the bait! . . .

Lucky for me that my captor saw how very young and small I was. After deciding I could not be used, I was let off the hook.

After that experience I should have known better! However, I just couldn't pass it up. So, I took the chance and hoped I wouldn't be caught. . . .

Oh, the heat didn't bother me much, but the idea of being assimilated was horrifying. Even so, I couldn't do anything about it.

Well, before I am no more, I would like to pass this bit of advice on to my captor and his associates: "Try to throw back all of us that are young and small. For it will only be a matter of time before they will become bigger and much better tasting fish like myself. Why, I will go so far as to recommend that you throw us all back (alive) as a project for conservation!"[10]

---

[10] This was written for English 9 in 1960.

WHAT TO DO

In the event of a nuclear attack, many of the houses shall not be safe. Some people may think that they will be safe in a church but most churches, if exposed to earthquake caused by a nuclear bomb, would collapse and even God could not prevent that. The best thing for all the Murphys and Schwartzes to do would be to clear out all the shelves and such that are in a corner of their basement, and use the corner for a bomb shelter for themselves, their women and children. To do this would be much safer than staying above ground, for the first thing to go would be all the roofs in town. Don't try to be heroes and worry about your sons-in-law, but worry about your own families, otherwise you may end up as so many sheep at the slaughter house.[11]

---

[11] This was written November 3, 1960. Since then, we know that no one would survive a nuclear blast that would take the roofs off of houses. We were given hope by a government that knew there was no hope. It was public relations.

Paragraph #1

Ah food, the substance that could allay the feeling of emptiness that fills the very depth of the pit within me; how it seems unattainable and forever lost. When will I be able to indulge to my utmost satisfaction? From within the emptiness, a voice of pain is calling: "Food! Food!" Oh but to fulfill the very wishes of the voice. It would be a heaven of bliss to appease this pang of hunger that eats away my previous feeling of fulfillment.[12]

---

[12] This was written on November 23, 1960.

PARAGRAPH #2

Mouse hunting is not as dangerous as rat hunting, but it has its thrills. I had awakened this morning with but one thought in my mind, "to catch a mouse." I moved from my abode and soon took a position behind a chair. Soon there came a mouse, scurrying by just out of reach. I followed it and discovered its hole. Finding a favorable offensive position was not difficult, for the television set was close by. I waited for what seemed like hours. Then I saw it! It poked its head out of the hole! My heart beat faster! I moved slowly. Cautiously it moved from the hole. I pounced! Ah, mice are delicious. For after all, I am a cat.[13]

---

[13] This was written on November 26, 1960.

A SPEECH

As most of you well know, I am up here, standing in front, with proper stance, attempting to look each of you in the eyes, with the noble and courageous task of informing you.

Now, if there are among you those who have rotten tomatoes as their form of criticism, I will refuse to proceed. . . .

Well, since my fears are groundless, I will now proceed . . . back to my desk.

How regrettable that this is not possible. This speech is quite essential to my fatalistic beliefs. Since you may not understand this term, I will define it.

I feel that the fates planned for me to give my speech at this time. Therefore, I must give it in accordance with my destiny. If I didn't, I don't believe that I would have any right to call myself a fatalist.

Do you realize that all of you have

your lives charted for you; each action on your part planned.

There have been numerous times when I might have been killed – but – because of my fate, I did not die and am not now cremated.

"Chance! Chance!"

Did I hear someone think?

No, it wasn't chance that I wasn't driving faster, didn't have a slower reaction, and didn't turn the wheel the right direction at the right time. It was fate; just fate.

Now that I have given you the only reason that I am now giving my speech, I shall continue.

In . . . Oh, I forgot something. How it fills me with chagrin. I forgot to give my speech before I explained my reasons for giving it. Now isn't that a twist of fate?[14]

---

[14] I sat down. This was the first speech I gave to the high school speech class. The teacher was not happy with me.

IT'S DISGRACEFUL

It's absolutely disgraceful! And did you know, did each of you know – you are being used!

Why, the whole system is nothing but a farce! Did you know that you aren't gaining a thing by going to school? Well, you don't. . . That is, nothing but knowledge.

Do you know what school is? School is a federal institution upheld for the sole purpose of ameliorating the unemployment problem. We are taught by jobless carpenters, mechanics, and common ditch diggers.

You ask why they teach. Besides being dedicated propagandists, they teach because they like to get paid for doing nothing. They teach everything that has been discarded by our predecessors. Our predecessors didn't learn a thing from them; and, confidentially, they flunked.

But even after proof that their

endeavor was to no avail, these "teachers" are still attempting to "brain wash" us into believing that an education would be an asset to us.

Why do we stand for this? Why don't we do something about it?

This unnecessary strain on brain tissue must stop! If we learn anything more, we won't be able to classify ourselves as ignorant – and this would be unbearable.

We must prevent this catastrophe! We must overthrow our oppressors!

Students of the world unite and stop learning![15]

---

[15] This is probably another one of my speeches from high school Speech class,

PET PEEVE

Pet peeve – I'm peeved all right, but I can't say that it's my pet. Day in and day out, it's always the same. What I wouldn't give for a glass of variety! Since you may question my use of the word, "glass", I should explain: I just thought that it to be a more appropriate measure than "bit of variety". – Not that it really matters, of course.

School, that's my peeve. I get up each morning, do the same thing before leaving for school, I ride the same bus, listen to the same teachers, eat lunch, listen to more teachers, and then go home. All of this is dreadfully boring and uninteresting.

There really isn't much to do about the whole mess – although there are a few possible cures.

We could abolish school, thus allowing us to grow into first class ignoramuses.

There is also a chance that a

mutation will come from the recent radiation in the atmosphere[16] that will enable an unborn child to learn all the knowledge he'll ever need while still in the womb.

Other than these two hopeful ideas, I don't believe there is any chance for a release from this torture. The only thing to do now is "grin and bear it."

---

[16] This speech was probably written in the fall of 1962 after the Russian nuclear tests in August and September of that year at Novaya Zemlya. A cloud of radiation was supposed to flow from there and go over the United States

YOU ARE MARKED

How many of you realize that you are marked. That some time or other in your life you will be approached. Now is the time to prepare yourself - to strengthen yourself against the plague of the devil.

I can guess your thoughts. You now believe that you are about to hear a sermon because I am a preacher's kid. Well, maybe you're right; and maybe you're wrong. But this is a warning to be cautious about any decision that is brought before you.

Have you ever thought of cheating? Has anyone ever asked you to cheat?

Here is a decision that must be made cautiously. One answer will bring you happiness, knowing that all you have done and achieved you have done alone.

The other is contagious. This answer to the big decision may influence your whole way of life. You may end by cheating on the gas mileage by driving a few miles an hour faster than is lawful. You may cheat yourself by getting a job for which you are really not qualified; thus being the first to be laid off.

If you have any desire at all for tranquility, you will take care; for the devil has many ways of renting you a hot home.

Now wait a minute, I'm not saying that those who cheat will end up in – in a hot house; but I do know that an ambassador for the devil has many, many ways of mulcting[17] you. There are various forms of him: temptation in your mind; temptation offered you by outside sources; and of course the usual form.

Oh, surely you know what his usual form is. You don't?

Well, I might as well give you a description. He is rather short and thin; he has kind eyes, a gentle expression, a soft voice; he likes loud colors, preferably red. Of course I mustn't

---

[17]Mulcting means fining or defrauding: to deprive (someone) of something, as by fraud, extortion, etc.; swindle, to obtain (money or the like) by fraud, extortion, etc. to punish (a person) by fine, especially for a misdemeanor. This may be the only time I ever used the word: mulcting. I can't remember why I used it.

forget his most important feature: He always wears a hat. Why? – Well, that reason should be obvious.

Do you realize that at this very moment at least one more person has fallen prey to this – this – creature!

It's absolutely disgraceful that people are so gullible and clay-minded.

Well, the only thing I can do about it is warn you: Watch out for the devil's ambassador, for some day, he may approach you.[18]

---

[18] This is another one of those speeches written in the fall of 1962.

A FABLE ABOUT
THE CUBAN MISSLE CRISIS[19]

We all knew that she had no real home, no real opportunities, but we ignored that fact.

Her father used her assets to set himself up in the world. He lent her out at fifty dollars an hour and kept all but what was needed to keep her desirable to her callers.

Most of the callers were basically vulgar barbarians who took part of her life away with them each time they left. Not one left her a part of his life, a crime that will destroy any woman's vivacity. During the day the wealthy callers were afraid to come and the girl sat alone in her father's walled courtyard without friends or any companion, for her father drummed up his night business at this time.

One day, a youth who was trimming trees saw her sitting alone, friendless.

---

[19] This was written in the spring of 1963.

He took his ladder and climbed over the wall. It was love at first sight, for him at least; the girl would have given him all the love and tenderness of which she was capable, but her father discovered them while they talked. He beat the youth badly and had him imprisoned with the charge: "attempted rape."

The youth told the story of the girl's sorry plight, but was paid no heed. Prominent citizens of the community were among the girl's callers and this made the whole situation rather touchy. These "honorable, upstanding" citizens would not take a stand against the wrong because they enjoyed having their hours with the girl.

Most other citizens, including the mayor, did not want to bring out the skeletons of the community and make enemies of those citizen-callers and lose face with the surrounding communities.

A few fearless citizens half-heartedly went to the girl's father and asked him to be good to his daughter; then they went to the youth during visiting hours and sympathized with him, but did little else.

An out-of-town-stranger, after hearing the story, posted bail for the young man. After several anxious days, the youth and his new friend found a way to get the father away from the house. The out-of-town-stranger posed as a rich, prospective client and lured the father away from the house. The father went readily, for he felt secure in his past authority.

Without the presence of her father, the young man gave the daughter a choice: marry him, be rid of her father, and better her position; or stay with the father and slowly continue her decadence. The daughter gladly consented to matrimony and she and her beau were soon legally bound.

The father returned to find his "golden goose" taken from his control. He was told in no uncertain terms to "get the hell out and stay out". He left but took with him the safely concealed fortune he had made in his former business.

The community publicly applauded

the girl's husband for pulling the girl out of the dirt; but her old callers privately cried over their loss.

Even with this change in her status, the community remained cool to the girl. They did not make the little effort to be friendly and helpful, but kept aloof, not giving them the opportunities that they had withheld before and that the couple now needed so badly.

The out-of-town-stranger was the couple's good friend. He told them things that could come to them in the future. The couple began to strive for the fulfillment of a dream, but things were happening too slowly. Many improvements had to be made immediately.

The wife was reluctant about the whole affair, but she trusted the judgment of her husband. So, when the out-of-town-stranger suggested that, since they could not get help from the community, they borrow the necessary money from him and get some things from his out-of-town-company, the husband decided to do so and the wife readily conformed.

The husband had a problem though. He didn't have much money and an income only from menial labor. He could not begin to pay the out-of-town-stranger for his generosity. Here again, the out-of-town-stranger had the solution. The husband's wife was beautiful and worth something. So the out-of-town-stranger moved in with the couple as a permanent caller. This was the way to meet payments.

When the community heard of this, they were appalled. They cried out against the husband and tried to get the marriage annulled, but that was impossible! The marriage was legal and the girl was of age. Then the mayor told the citizens to stop dealing with them, to ostracize them.

This was done and the husband could not buy food in their groceries, buy medicine in their drugstores, or buy gas from their gasoline stations. The poor man was even fired from his job. This did not help matters; the couple just became more dependent on the out-of-town-stranger.

Since they saw the failure of this method, the prominent citizens of the community, among them many of the girl's former callers, hired some men who with the aid of a number of volunteers, attempted to put the husband out of the house bodily, or end his life.

This did not work, for the husband had hired body guards at the out-of-town-stranger's suggestion, paying for them in the usual manner.

There are a great many more people in the community; and out there, there is more money and brute strength. The community could easily use its superior force to destroy the husband and drive the out-of-town-stranger from the premises. Would this be wrong?

The lot of the wife is better. Granted, she has a hard time; but before, she had a father who may have loved her, yet his addiction to avarice was terrible. He used her shamefully for his own material gain.

Now, a husband, who probably

loves her, is using her to achieve improvements in their lot. The husband is forgetting the value of morals; yet too, the wife may not mind the sacrifices she is making for something that seems worthwhile.

If the community is so interested in the girl's welfare, why didn't it do something about her deplorable condition under the guardianship of her father? Now they don't like the couple's arrangement with the out-of-town-stranger.

The community is angered that an alien is taking advantage of the couple, especially the girl. Why weren't they angered to the point of doing something about the situation when the callers had been citizens of the community? If the community is so conscientious, it could flood the couple with gifts and aid in attempt to increase their influence with them and hope to bring them out of the clutches of the out-of-town-stranger. But will it do that?

Something of this sort would be expensive in economic terms and, possibly, in prestige. The community would have to admit it was wrong in the first place, that it did not do its duty. It seems that the community has a tendency to be egotistical. Could it ever admit that it is fallible?

Even if the community did this, it may be too late, for even whores and charlatans can have pride; yet, better too late than never.

The community could very easily give aid and assistance to the couple without condemning and punishing. An action of this kind would be admirable for its helpfulness and purpose. It may result in the husband sending the out-of-town-stranger packing; in the wife legally divorcing her husband on the grounds of mental and physical cruelty; or the wife threatening to leave unless her husband throws the out-of-town-stranger out on his ear. Even if this does not happen, it is the girl's choice. She is of age.[20]

---

[20] After I wrote this, the teacher of my high school government class (1962-63) suggested that I send it to Esquire Magazine. I typed it for submission but I never sent it to them.

THE PROPHET

The prophet is a visionary with many pet ideas. Living inside him is hope and idealism. When he begins to prophesy, the little beasties wiggle out, slowly, one at a time.

But eventually, if he is allowed to continue, the snakes wiggle up from inside his hopeful imagination and burst out of his mouth all at once; tumbling over each other and entangling everything.[21]

---

[21] I wrote this; making fun of prophets while in a class about the Prophets and their times at Otterbein College in 1964.

ONCE A FERN, ALWAYS A FROND

As the reed ever whispered
The secret of Midas' ears;
So the fossil fern
Forever tells this tale:

Limbo! For these eons I have been in Limbo – pleasantly recalling the soft winter breeze blowing through the sieve of my fingers, savoring the heat of sunshine warming my open palm; experiencing over and over again the pleasant sensations of the life that was mine. All was pleasant to me; never was I shocked from my reverie.

When the heat of sunshine slowly faded at nightfall, I gave each visiting breeze some warmth to take away. The breeze was better for having touched my skin. Before morning and the creeping out of sunshine to kiss my palm again, the dew gathered about my fingers bathing me until I nodded in dreamy appreciation, almost soothed to sleep.

Always it was, as the glow spread across the eastern horizon, that the night and I were one in temperature; then began again, the gentleness of all my previous days.

Of the cause of my present state, I recall only the shadow of a hulk which lumbered near. Then it was I entered Limbo with my memories.[22]

---

[22] I wrote this on April 22, 1965 for second year English in College. I think this was the start of another short story that I never finished.

AUTO-SKETCH-A-WOOLYWORM[23]

Once upon a time, there was a caterpillar with fuzz all around. He sort of climbed up and down eating leaves and stretching from twig to twig. He crawled and crawled, exploring while he ate until late in his first night, he found himself a corner and isolated his involvement.

He was entombed, cocooned, protected from the outside cold, and hot and warm and wet and dry; locked up in willed exile, imposed to self, without a thought.

Forever it seemed he'd be there. Year after year passed by when other caterpillars were flying by. He felt too well off and too confused to venture more; for in climbing round and round and up and down, he'd never seen the whole tree; just its parts.

So there he sat or lay without a need for out there knowing; it seemed,

---

[23] Auto (Ought to) sketch a wooly worm; another play on words; meaning a self-portrait.

faintly unaware the best to be was inside, away from dragging, climbing and crawling. All his culture had been born to climb and eat and crawl and search and find scraps of things but never see the whole.

Then once he thought: "What the hell – a caterpillar wasn't good, albeit, but a cocoon is worse - unless you're dead, why fill a grave? I ought to be involved again."

So out he sprang - a flutterby[24] - and saw the tree as a whole and was blown away! But now as calm has set the overpowering wind of growth: the winging butterfly has flowers in mind to light upon and visit a spell.

Love,

Guess who?[25]
(My address then.)

---

[24] When I was writing letters or poetry, I loved to mix up the letters in words such as the above: "fl" and "b".

[25] I think I wrote this to a friend from college who is referred to as a flower. It would have been while I was in Seminary: January1967- June1970. It was the Seminary's old address that would have been between the parentheses. This was an apology for not writing sooner and in a timely manner.

'BYE LINE

Deep in the ever protective jungle of blackboards and towered halls[26], a scholarly community struggled mightily to bring upon itself the blessings of a liberal education. And the struggle was mighty for the consistence of the community was only a quantity of apes and an assortment of mild mannered intellectual monkeys.

In the jungle school (where the banana is a sign of infinity), the professors were forever aping upon the students the necessity of concentrating their efforts for the attainment of a liberal education, but that education appeared to be just another case of monkey see, monkey do.

Also living in that community was Superape. Disguised as a mild mannered intellectual monkey, he would withdraw from society to prevent thought crimes and other abortive attempts at

---

[26] This is in reference to Towers Hall, a building on the Otterbein College campus.

individualism. The only grave danger he ever saved the community from occurred thus:

It was evening. The breeze was blowing a trumpet softly through the trees and no other sound could be heard, for it was study day. The community was on the lawn quietly grazing through their text books in a valiant effort to ingest all the information therein before the coming examinations. Suddenly an odd cry was heard.

"Is it that schizoid Superape sometimes disguised as a mild mannered intellectual monkey trying to get our attention again?" asked one scholar as he hung from a branch by his tail with a portion of Charles Darwin's Origin of the Species hanging from the corner of his mouth.

"No," said another scholar, burping slightly as he washed down a Pauline epistle with Blatz.[27]

---

[27] This was a brand of beer commonly found in the fraternity houses at Otterbein College.

"Let us go and see what it is that we have heard," said one to another, "if it is not but the breeze blowing wind through the trees."

It was not but the breeze blowing and so the community rose as one into the trees and peered through the foliage and saw the creator of the sound. It was an animal, a donkey.

"We shall make him our mascot, the symbol of our scholastic endeavor," cried the community in one voice, "We shall call his – her – its name, 'Democrat!'"

And at that moment, a mild mannered intellectual monkey flung himself out of a tree and plunged to the ground, attempting to fly. It was Superape. Having the attention of the community, he said from the ground: "Thou shouldst not call the name of the donkey, 'Democrat' for thou art not a political community; and thou shouldst have nothing to do with the world."

And all heard the wisdom of his dying words and believe he was schizoid and they changed the name of the donkey forthwith. They called him – her – it, "Asinine."

From "Assorted Jungle Tales"
By Robinson Kipling[28]

---

[28] This was probably written in 1965 when I complained about the dress code required to enter the student center dining room.

THE SACRED AND THE PROFANE
(Plaque before the entrance
of the forest temple)

Read hereon, anthropoids that thou might need to know what thou shouldst do to preserve the sanctity of this, thy institution:

Thou shouldst not enter here with gleeful heart, for thou dost profane by thy glee the sobriety of the institution: Education is a somber affair.

Thou shouldst not enter here unshod for if thy toes be dirty (read Catch 22) thou wouldst profane the institution by thy uncleanliness.

Thou shouldst not enter here in such attire as wouldst direct the attention of the forest guard upon thine self. Thou shouldst wear such as to appear an integral part of the scene: Camouflage thy individuality. If thou shouldst appear as the very walls themselves, thou shouldst sanctify thy very entrance within the institution.

True, walls have ears, but no mouth. Listen and learn but do not speak thy mind for thy mind is foul, filled with thy profanities, thy questions, thy confusion.

Thy tail shouldst never be shown, nor thy dirty linen, nor thy smirks. Thou art only a member of the community and shouldst not do what wouldst not be done in the light of the above regulations.

Bow thy head, knob thy horns, retract thy fore-claws, and close thy mouth. Enter, thou blest, into the sanctity of this, thy loving institution.

Anthropoid read and believe. Do not question.[29]

---

[29] I wrote this about the college dress code in the dining room of the Student Center at Otterbein College in 1965.

CONVERSATION WITH AN
M.S.G.B. CAT

"Hey, Cat!"

"Yowl."

"Remember that ballot stuffed in the off-campus mail boxes last week?

"Yowl."

"Well, I voted. I marked an 'X' before one name just like I was supposed to."

"Yowl. That's good. It's good to see someone interested enough to take the time to vote."

"That's what I thought, Cat. But I shouldn't have bothered."

"Yowl. Why? Didn't the man you voted for win? That's just like all the rest of you. You don't vote and complain about who wins and then you vote and complain about who wins. That's typical."

"Now, wait a minute, Cat. I mean that when you get a ballot and you are supposed to vote, isn't there supposed to be a ballot box where you put your ballot after you vote?"

"Yowl, and there was one; down in the information office."

"Like hell there was."

"Yowl. Now hold on, you can't talk to me like that. I'm on the Men's Student Government Board. We are a responsible organization. You are just sore because the man you wanted didn't win."

"Cat, I checked the information office. The ballot was in my mailbox and I voted at 8:40 A.M. I looked for the ballot box. I went upstairs. I went downstairs. I went upstairs and I checked with the information office and the lady said, and I quote, 'They haven't given the ballot box to us yet. Why don't you keep your ballot until later?' So put your money where your mouth is." Cat didn't have any money. "By the way, Cat."

"Yowl."

"I voted anyway. I dropped my ballot into the waste basket."[30]

---

[30] I wrote this about Otterbein College in 1965.

TELE – MICRO – SCOPE

Recess is over and class resumes. The teacher says, "I see that you are confused by the two words 'microscope' and 'telescope'. We will have a short vocabulary lesson."

The teacher goes to the blackboard and begins to write as she talks. "The root of both words is 'scope'. It means 'to see' or 'to view'. The prefixes 'tele' and 'micro' mean 'far' and 'small' respectively. What do you get when you combine these prefixes with the root?"

We do as we are told and attain "telemicroscope" or "microtelescope".

The teacher looks over our shoulders at our work. Storming to the front, she says, "No! You are doing it all wrong!"

The small boy in the front row retorts innocently, "We did exactly as you said."

Our teacher stops to think for a moment. After careful thought, she says, "Take two roots and add a prefix to each of them. You should result in 'telescope' or microscope'. What do these two words mean?"

One of the back row boys says, "'See far – 'view small'!"

The little boy in the front row inquires, "Aren't they instruments - things?"

"Yes, that's right," the teacher agrees, "Can someone tell us more about these two instruments?" She looks down the rows searching for a likely suspect – a person who knows the answer and is trying to hide it behind a blank face. "Ginger?" the teacher calls.

A pretty miss who looks as intelligent as the ultra-feminine blondes on television loses her vacant look. She takes an extra-deep breath and releases it in a long sigh. "A telescope," she begins, "is an optical aid used by astronomers to study large, distant bodies."

Someone interrupts the girl with a snicker and this accompanying whisper: "Bodies like Venus – when the curtain's not drawn."

The teacher squelches any forthcoming laughter with a cold stare. Then she throws out her chin and puts her hands on her hips and says, "That is not a thought for third-graders!"

Unconcernedly her eyes move to center on Ginger and she urges, "Go on."

Ginger takes another deep breath and looks at the two boys sitting on each side of her without turning her head. She releases the air in another sigh and continues, "A microscope is nearly homogeneous to a telescope in structure, but it is used by biologists to study infinitesimally small microbes – germs!"

"Thank you, Ginger!" says the teacher, spitting the words out from behind a Cheshire-cat smile, in Lawrence-Welk style.

The girl lifts her nose just slightly before she resumes a blank face similar to that on her surrounding peers.

The teacher, with all masterly pride, asks without hesitation, "Are there any questions?"

"Yes," says the boy in the front row, "how do they work?"[31]

_____

[31] I wrote this for an Education 101 assignment in the spring of 1966.

PHONE ETTIQUETTE

Jill was talking over by the coke machine, hanging onto the telephone cord with her feet and dangling the business end in front of her mouth by her left paw. After a few minutes of talking gaily, she stopped suddenly and listened. Then with a horrible shriek, she hung up the phone.

She lay down on the sofa pillow holding her head. She was gently so gently massaging her ear with her fingertips. All the girls gathered around.

She kept moaning, "I've been raped! I've been raped!" over and over again.

Several of the girls tried to hold her and touch her ear – because the way she touched it – it was giving her a great deal of pain. Every time she moved, she favored her ear just a little – not moving too fast or too sharply so as to pull or jerk her auditory canal.

After a while, she calmed down. Someone bought her a coke and like giddy vultures waiting for a bit of juicy gossip to guzzle, we all waited for her to tell us what happened.

Eventually someone of us asked, "What happened?"

Jill moved slightly away from that girl and touched her ear with her little finger so gently. She said, "I've just been raped."

We all move a little bit closer – someone accidentally bumped Jill and she held her head again in pain – or something.

Several girls chimed, "Come on, Jill, tell us how it happened!"

"Well," she said, "this groovy guy was talking to me about going on a date. He wanted to take me down to the dam tonight. You know. Well, I told him there were a lot of places I'd go with him, you know: movie, opera house, theater, Charlie's Place. But I couldn't go to the dam because I considered myself a virgin and, even though I liked him an awful lot, I just didn't want to get into a position I couldn't get out of; and that I knew what it was like; I was there once before. The only thing that saved me was that the guy had forgotten to bring a rubber and . . ."

She kept talking on and on and on, getting more excited and breathy all the time.

Eventually Jill said, "I did tell him that I would so much like to go to the Lodge with him since I knew he was such a good dancer. Then he said, 'Hold it! Hold it!' I didn't hear him for a minute, finally he said very loud, 'Jill, shut up!'"

She stopped talking. We all waited.

She said, "Then it happened! He did it. He said very calmly, very patiently, and tenderly and carefully; but never letting up on his masculine forcefulness and penetrating personality. He said, 'Jill, fuck you.' And he hung up."

We all looked at each other in utter and perfect astonishment.

While we sat with mouths agape in a double take, Jill said, holding her ear, "I've been raped. It hurts, but it feels so good."

Egad!

Well, that's Jill, from ear to ear the same.[32]

---

[32] This was written about 1965. I was being a little playful with a particular word.

COME HERE CHILD

Pietro Santillini stroked the canvas with his brush. The Magnificat draped in white stood in the garden, dutifully the handmaiden of God. He had painted her face with a look of simple purity – the naïve face of the Virgin. Pietro lay his brush aside.

Suppose she hadn't been a virgin. Pietro thought. Suppose the Mother of God had been a whore.

The thought pleased him. He felt it would serve the fools right if she had lain with a man in that garden. Pietro closed his eyes to visualize the rape of a willing Virgin. Wouldn't he love to have been that man: a centurion, a childhood playmate, or a traveling merchant? The thought aroused him.

Pietro opened his eyes; he did not look at the painting; he looked at the model. He did not see her as his contemporary. He saw her as the embodiment of the Virgin in his painting. He licked his lips.

He called to her, "Come here, child."

The young girl stepped from the block and came to where he sat. His right hand stroked the cloth the old woman had draped about her. The old woman would have followed his order.

Pietro moved aside one fold of cloth and place the flat of his right palm upon the Virgin's naked belly. The girl's breath caught in surprise. Pietro did not look up at her face. He knew what it was like. Her eyebrows would be lifted; her eyes wide with surprise. Her mouth would be hanging loosely open in a small "O" of astonishment.

Pietro moved his right hand caressingly along her stomach and tightened it against her hip. Her eyebrows would be lifted no longer; her eyes would be half-closed in satisfaction. Her mouth would yet be hanging loosely open, but the corners would be turned up by a half-smile of pleasure. Pietro drew the other fold of cloth aside and placed his left hand upon her other hip.

Holding her steady with both hands, he pressed his lips to her vulva in a kiss.

Slowly Pietro stood up, bringing his hands up along her ribcage to keep the folds of cloth apart. His hands slid from her armpits to cup each of her breasts with a palm. He did not look at the girl's face, but down between the folds of cloth and at her feet. His gaze gradually climbed her beautiful legs and rested upon her thighs. She had twisted them apart, instinctively, allowing for easier entry.

Pietro smiled and brought his gaze up higher. His gaze hesitated a moment at her navel and then continued upward. He moved his hands so that the palms were no longer pressed against her nipples and his hands could squeeze each of her breasts into a peak. He bent down and took each nipple into his mouth sucking on it gently.

The girl moaned in pleasure each time she felt his mouth on one of her nipples.

With one hand and its elbow, Pietro kept the two folds of cloth apart and from falling off of her shoulders. He reached down with his free hand and released his confined penis; it sprang outward like a switchblade. Pietro did not look at her face; nor did he need to; as he stepped in against her, she pressed her face into the curvature of his neck and chin. He felt the hot breath of her moan as the sword entered its sheath.

Pietro kept the cloth from falling as he bent her backward to lay with him upon the floor.

Pietro could visualize himself held against the heated body of a young Jewess. He laughed as they reached climax together. He laughed in the face of God.[33]

---

[33] In high school I thought of writing historical fiction. This was one of the ideas I planned to embellish when I had the time. It is based upon a real person. Spaniard: Murillo (1617-1682) who painted the Immaculate Conception at least fifteen times. His models were young girls of Seville that his paintings would surround with the idealism of the teachings of the church. I thought he might have had a hidden motive and some theological issues to work out; my plan was to tell in detail a fictionalized account of the seduction of each one of his models and conjecture about his love/hate relationship with God. There were many projects like this one. I never had the time to finish them and now I have lost interest.

ONLY ONE MONTH FULL GROWN

Davy was only eighteen and not at all as worldly as he claimed to be. Having graduated from high school just last month, he felt he'd only had one month of freedom and growth to real maturity.

It was Wednesday, the fifteenth of July to be exact. Davy was vacationing with his family at a lake resort section of Michigan. He'd been traveling for three days and found nothing at all exciting about his adulthood and newly gained privileges so far.

His family had arrived early that evening. After helping to unpack and get everyone situated in the family cabin, Davy had asked for the car so he could look around. Without comment or a time deadline, his father had handed him the car keys. Immediately, Davy headed for Bill's Dusk to Dawn Café. He arrived shortly after eleven.

When Davy stepped inside and took

a look around he knew there were no girls there. Of course, Davy remembered the rumors he'd heard in the past of Bill's backroom upstairs, so he wouldn't have sworn there weren't any women in the building. At any rate, there were none in sight.

Davy sat down at the bar and ordered a beer. The bartender smiled at Davy's youthful face and produced the beer. Davy set the price down and picked up the bottle and a glass and went to a corner stall. Davy sat down next to the window and peered out at the night. Only six cars were parked in the near-empty parking lot. Davy poured his beer into the glass and then settled into the far corner of the bench; leaning the back of his head against the window, he surveyed the inside of the café.

The bartender was sitting in a chair and leaning back against the wall behind him. Two fellows were down at one end of the bar in a drinking contest. The two men were on their fourth beer and discussing the Republican National

Convention. The door behind the bar opened and Davy saw the poolroom and three men playing poker. There were stairs going up to the second floor in that room. No one was playing pool. The man that had opened the door caught the bartender's eye.

The bartender got off of his chair and came to the customer.

The man holding the door open smiled and said, "Bill would you bring us four beers, please."

Bill, the owner and bartender smiled and said, "Comin' right up, Jack!"

The door closed behind Jack.

Davy looked down at his untouched beer. He picked it up. He tried to prepare his stomach for what he knew was inevitable. He raised the glass to his lips and took a quick swallow.

The taste never bothered him when he swallowed quickly, but it didn't help his stomach any. He sighed and decided he'd better just sip the beverage slowly.

Maybe, he thought, I'll try whiskey again – if I can get this down.

A car pulled into the parking lot and

his attention was turned to the other side of the window.

In the glow of the car's ceiling light, Davy could see a pretty brunette. He waited expectantly for the driver to go to the other side of the car and open the door for his date. The driver didn't. He came into the café, asked for a six-pack of cold beer, and went out.

Davy watched disappointedly as the car drove the pretty brunette out of sight.

Davy looked down at his drink. He was surprised to find his glass empty and the bottle empty. He looked up toward the bartender and found Bill's eyes already on him.

Davy asked for a whiskey. Bill shook his head and then brought Davy another beer and collected payment.

The two men at the end of the bar were now on their fifth bottle of beer. They were maudlin now as they recalled the orgy their high school basketball team had the night before the championship game. They had won their game the next afternoon but had been trounced that evening.

The clock above the door of the café read three o'clock. The men in the poker game had just ordered more refreshment. The two men at the bar had fallen asleep at two thirty without either of them finishing his fifth beer.

Davy was sipping his third beer and still hoping for some excitement. Shortly another car drove into the parking lot and a young couple climbed out of the car.

The young lady was almost beautiful as she stepped through the doorway and into the café. Her date, who had held the door, was a rather nice looking fellow with dark hair and blue eyes. He followed the young lady's lead as she sat down in a stall next to the one Davy was in.

Davy had noticed her too blonde hair, but overlooked that because she had such a well-formed figure.

Davy was beginning to think that maybe the night wouldn't be so dull after all. But, thirty minutes later, no other cars had shown up, no women had emerged from the backroom, and the young couple was getting along famously.

With a sigh of regret, Davy stood up to his full five-foot, eleven and a half inch height and stretched. He remembered he'd promised his younger brother to go fishing with him at six o'clock the next morning. If he headed home now, he would get at least two hours of sleep.

Davy turned to look once more at the pretty fake-blonde before he left. She was looking at his muscular one-hundred-and-sixty-pound figure.

She looked at Davy's handsome face and her eyes were full of her frank admiration for this slender Tarzan.

Whether Davy noticed the look in her eyes is hard to say, but the young woman's date was instantly aware of her expression.

The woman's blue-eyed date stood up and turned to stand face to face with Davy. The fellow towered over Davy by at least one inch, but this didn't seem to matter anymore than the fellow's fifty more pounds to Davy.

The bartender was quite aware of what could happen between two willing roosters. He thought very quickly. Bill took up a tray and put two glasses of wine on it. Then he quietly walked up to the two young men as they were looking each other over.

"Pardon me, gentlemen!" Bill said. He looked up at the blue-eyed husky and said, "Your order of wine."

The husky sat back down and Bill served the two glasses. When he stood up, Bill noticed the disappointed look written all over Davy's face.

Very courteously, Bill said, "Good night!"

Davy sighed and shrugged his shoulders before saying, "Good night."

As Davy drove back to his family's cabin, he snorted to himself, "That café didn't live up to its reputation."

Thursday morning was a miserable time for Davy. He went fishing with his brother as he had promised, but caught nothing. It was too hot for fishing and the morning-after hangover didn't do anything to ease his misery.

By lunchtime, when the younger boy finally tired of feeding the fish with the bait from his hook, Davy was feeling so low that he went right back to bed. He didn't eat lunch or even drink a glass of water.

Davy slept soundly until past supper time. Then he got up and had cold ham sandwiches with milk.[34]

---

[34] This was written in 1964 during the Republican National Convention.

THE LAB RAT

How incredible, I thought, to think that for all these years I have never been out of this room.

I had never really thought about the outside before. I know that I had grown restless several months ago. It was then that I began to look at my small environment with questions and a new interest.

Every morning for as long as I can remember, I had the same schedule. I awoke early, washed, ate a breakfast, and then went to the view screen where I watched a man or, sometimes, a woman talk about my lessons. I wrote letters; took tests, grading myself; and read all the numerous books, magazines and pamphlets that always filled the library in the corner. After I had read these, a new supply replaced them.

The way that I received new reading material had been a mystery that I could not solve; that is, until now.

I ate lunch which, in recent years, I

had been preparing for myself. Shortly after lunch, I would return to the view screen and resume my lessons.

After another hour or two, I would begin physical exercises, move on to Taekwando, and end with a session of yoga. My instructions for all of these were on the view screen.

Upon the completion of this portion of the day, I would eat a self-prepared supper following a menu I found on a small bulletin board. Afterwards, I would wash the dishes; another task I had recently begun to perform regularly.

With this accomplished, I would read books, return to the view screen for entertainment, or I would try to think. The latter I had been doing much of late.

When I was tired, I would bathe and retire. On the morn, I would repeat the same thing.

As I have already stated, until recently, I had been quite willing to conform to my rigid schedule.

One mid-morning several months ago, I was watching one of my usual educational programs when a realization that must have been in my sub-conscious mind for several years came to the surface.

I had never seen another human being in the flesh. They had always been on the view screen.

At first I laughed it off, but soon I was really thinking deeply for the first time in my life. I thought that there was a possibility that I was the only being left alive after a war over a petty circumstance had destroyed mankind.

After that idea came to me, I began to calm down and I tried to imagine the happenings that had led to my confinement here. This of course did not keep me secure for long; for I soon realized that the new literature that was always provided must come from some human source. With that one thought, I began to understand and remember other similar things that I had taken for granted.

I soon began to feel that I needed more time to think than I had now; especially since my attention was actually divided. With this, I turned my full attention on the view screen and followed my complete schedule to the evening.

By evening, I was almost frantic, mentally. I soon settled into a favorite chair, shut my eyes and prayed that I would not go insane.

Shortly, having composed the turmoil in my mind, I began to evaluate, rationally, my status within and without my environment.

I soon began to understand that all knowledge wasn't mine; that within this small environment, there were things happening that I didn't know any thing about.

With this realization, I broadened my thoughts and began to think of reasons for these mysterious happenings. Barring no possible reasons, I categorized and listed them in my mind.

Upon retiring, I told myself that the only way I could possibly discover the truth was to keep my mind awake and active at all times. Then I let my body rest while I learned to listen and keep my mind alert.

During the next couple of days, I followed my usual routine completely during the day; and at night I kept aware of every sound and every movement of air that touched the hairs on my head and arms.

It wasn't until the third eve of my initiative to vigil that I had the call. It was a low mental call asking me questions. Of course, I answered mentally and made no attempts to think anything else but the answers.

After a couple of months of training, I felt the slightest movement of air. It alerted me to listen as carefully as possible. And then I heard a sound; a slight brushing sound of a book or books sliding onto a shelf. I had heard this sound many times when I was its source.

I felt elation for quite a few days after hearing that one sound. Of course, there were more detectible sounds after that one; but it was the first sound that gave me for the first time a sense of elation that stayed with me: Knowing, by my own senses, that there was another creature, besides myself, that had contact with this environment.

On many occasions, I attempted to discern, without actual contact with the source, the way through which other beings came into my abode; that, I was unable to accomplish.

Several months after that wonderful enlightenment, I had a plan that I felt would secure my deliverance. As the day progressed, I felt more and more that I should not make the attempt. But I conquered these fears by telling myself that I must do it soon for another opportunity might never occur.

With the advent of my afternoon of physical activity, my last bit of anguish was quelled. I allowed myself to collapse after my last jump and spin during my Taekwando lesson.

I lay there motionless with my eyes open and fixed to an immovable object. I hoped that I looked as if I were ill to my observers. I had come to the conclusion that I was being observed.

As I lay still, I checked over in my mind, the list of preparations that I had made: I had a number of cubes of carbohydrate nourishment in my pocket; and I was wearing clothes that a young man had been wearing on one of the programs that I had seen on the view screen. I got much satisfaction out of noting that I had followed my list and plan to the most incidental detail.

I know that I must have laid still for an hour or more. My anxiety was building, but I kept it a bay by using my yoga slow breathing exercises and I did not move from where I fell.

Eventually I heard an almost inaudible whispering sound. I felt a very slight draft. And then I saw out of the corner of my stationary view, figures standing above me. As they drew closer, I noticed that they wore hoods and masks that were similar to those worn by the instructors in my anatomy program.

I picked out a victim, the white-clad figure nearest the usually hidden door into my environment. Almost before they could wink, I, in what seemed to be one continuous motion, arose, grasped the chosen figure around the neck, and choked it into submission as I carried it through the doorway out of my prison. (By then, I was certain that I was in a prison or a science laboratory of sorts.)

It wasn't until after I had done all of this that cries of dismay began to be uttered by a number of the other figures that I had avoided in my flight. While they raised the alarm, I ran through one door and then another. I am certain that the second door would have been closed and locked if they had not responded to the fake emergency that I had created.

As I came out into a large room, larger than my own abode, I saw other beings, some not clad in white and many others that were. For a moment I was amazed at the appearance of these, but knowing that my only chance of escape was to keep moving, I took a quick survey of the larger room I was in.

There were no windows anywhere.

(It was odd that I should think about windows at that moment.) Through another bigger doorway, I saw a long, vacant hallway; and at the end of that hallway was an "Exit" sign with an arrow pointing to the left. It was this route that I chose.

Moving swiftly and knocking one foolhardy chap out of my way, I ran down the long hall carrying my hostage. When I turned the corner, I collided with a couple of armed men running toward the room I had just left. Very easily, I put them to sleep with the back of my hand. Leaving them lying on the floor, I continued to run down this longer hallway toward a set of double doors with an exit sign above them.

As I ran, two men came through the double doors. They knelt and brought up rifles and aimed at me.

I used both arms to reposition my hostage for better protection. One of the men fired his rifle and I moved my hostage again to protect me from the shot.

I heard a thunk and saw a dart

resting in the back of my hostage. By then I was within reach of the two men with rifles.

Using my legs, I jumped and kicked each of the men in the head with my feet. Right foot hit the man on the right; and left foot hit the man on the left. They went down. I landed on top of them with both feet and went through the double door.

I was outside. Immediately I was astonished. I said aloud, "A sun! What had they done to me? All these years they had kept me out of sunlight."

I had no time to stop and look, aghast. I had to win my freedom. I looked around and I saw a way to go. It would take me down a sidewalk, across a street, and into the woods on the other side.

Many hours later, tired and puzzled, I sat before a small fire concealed by the rocks I had piled around it. I was far into the wooded hills that surrounded the small group of buildings where I had been imprisoned. I had moved my camp several times as searching parties got too close to me. My camp was now in the lee of two hills overlooking a small valley below.

I felt reasonably safe. I would hear anyone approaching me from either side or behind me; and I would see anyone approaching me from below.

I looked over at the figure of my hostage lying on the grass and the bed of soft boughs I had fixed. She was now breathing easily. It wasn't the labored breathing that had worried me after she was shot with the dart.

While I had been carrying her, I had come to the conclusion that my hostage was a woman. As I ran with her in my arms, I would reposition her every once in a while to relieve my aching muscles. I had felt the roundedness of her breasts through her clothing.

The first time I stopped to rest for a moment, I had removed her mask and hood. I had found that she was rather young; and if I could be classed as having any judgment as to beauty; I thought she was quite pretty.

I moved over toward her. As I had suspected, she was awake. I knew this by the way she shrank away at my approach.

I smiled at this and asked her, "Are you comfortable?"

There was no answer. I frowned.

What language had I spoken?

I thought for a moment, repeating my words in my head.

I had spoken in English.

I asked her the same question in each of the languages that I could speak: French first; and then German; followed by Spanish; and then Russian. But on each occasion, I received no answer. This puzzled me. Of course there were Finish, Swedish, and a few others, but I only knew how to translate them.

At length, a trembling voice issued from the prone figure. "I – I – I speak English," she swallowed audibly and then said, "I am quite comfortable."

Knowing that she was thoroughly frightened, I did not question her anymore. I said, "I am glad. I bid you good night." As I moved away from her, I added, "Sleep well."

Remaining vigilant the rest of the night, I mused over the happenings of the day.

I watched my first sunrise that morning. I had been too occupied with my exodus to watch the sunset.

As I watched the exquisite splendor, I voiced my thoughts. I said, "Just to see this, I would have given my life."

Happiness brought tears to my eyes.

I said, "Those damnable creatures; to know that they kept me from seeing this."

For the first time, I felt tears stream down my cheeks. I asked, "How can human beings be that inhumane?"

I heard a twig snap behind me. I turned quickly toward it to see my hostage backing away from me.

When she saw me turn toward her, she turned around and began to run away. She tripped.

Almost as she tripped, I had caught

up with her. I helped her to her feet and she desolately walked back to the camp ahead of me.

Upon reaching camp, I motioned for her to sit down, which she did.

I said, "Miss or Madame, if I were assured that I had a name, I would be delighted to introduce myself as 'Jim Brown' or whatever."

Her lips quivered as she looked into my eyes with wonder and that same fear I had noticed last night. I smiled at her.

She bit her lower lip and turned her head away.

I said, "You spoke to me last night. Aren't you going to say anything this morning?'

She said, dryly, "Hello."

I said, "I must apologize. If you hadn't been where you were yesterday, you wouldn't be here now."

She didn't say anything after that statement.

I sighed and looked again at the sunrise now passing.

Several minutes passed by before another sound was uttered. Then she spoke. She asked, "Why did you run away?"

I said, "Run away!" Then I laughed, bitterly.

She blushed and restated her question, "Why did you escape then?"

I looked right into her eyes. They were a dark blue.

I asked softly, "Wouldn't you?"

She didn't answer, but turned away and looked down into the small valley below.

At length, after quite a bit of mental conflict which showed on her face as she sat there, she turned her now saddened blue eyes on me, swallowed, took a deep breath, and then she said, "Your name is Alec Stanton Downs."

She shut her eyes, swallowed again, and then continued, "You are twenty-seven years old, seventy one and a half inches tall, and you weigh one hundred and sixty-five pounds."

Now she looked up at me again and said, "Your parents, if they had known about you, they would not have allowed it." She looked at me with pity in her eyes and said, "Your conception took place in a test tube. You were . . ."

I stopped whatever she was going to say by grabbing her head between the palms of my two hands. I held her head tightly and looked into her eyes. I said, "You're joking, aren't you?" I was hopeful, ready to laugh.

She said very sorrowfully, "I am sorry."

I released my hold on her head and turned away from her. I said, "Then, legally, I am not actually alive."

She said softly, "That's right."

I walked away from her. At the moment, I didn't care if she ran away or not. I sat down on a wide rock in front of a boulder and leaned my head back against the boulder.

From there, I asked, "May I have the remainder of the data?"

She looked into my expressionless face and smiled. She walked over and sat down beside me and leaned her head back against the boulder behind us.

We sat there in silence for a moment or two, then I asked, "Can you tell me about the two people who, I suppose, unknowingly, furnished the zygote from whence I came?"

She answered, "I don't know who they are or where they are, but I can tell you that they were ideal donors both physically and mentally."

I asked, "Were they intellectuals?"

She said, "Do you mean, well educated?"

I answered, "Yes."

She said, "They were that."

I said, "Not much else is there?"

She answered, "There are more details in the file at the Center."

I asked, "Center?"

She said, "The building where you were kept."

I said, "I understand." A question was forming in my mind. I asked, "Is the man who donated the sperm named Downs?"

She answered, "Not that I know of. You were named by the man who initiated the project.

I asked, "What is his name?"

She answered, "Stanton. Winthrop

Stanton."

I turned and looked down into her eyes.

She now looked at me with interest, not with the previous fear.

I turned my head away and looked up into the glorious blue sky.

Thinking aloud, I said softly with pleasure in my whole being, "There is so much that I have missed."

She whispered, "Pardon?"

I ignored her momentarily, and then I asked, "I noticed that the sun is in the southern sky. That shows that we are in the northern hemisphere. Just where, I don't know. Would you tell me exactly where I am?"

She answered, "You are somewhere on the North American continent. At a research center located in a forest preserve."

I asked, "Are there any roads into this area?"

"Yes, there is one to the west of the research center."

I said, "It doesn't go to the research center?"

She said, "No, it doesn't."

"How far away is it?"

She answered, "We're already west of the research center, aren't we?"

I said, "That's right."

"Well," she said, "It's approximately fifty-three miles from the center; as the crow flies."

I frowned at this, not understanding the colloquial term she used, but almost simultaneously, knowing its meaning.

I said, "Then we must get started going that way."

Without a word, she rose and began to move westward.

I said, "Wait a minute, miss. I must cover these embers with soil."

She asked, "Why?"

As I bent down to cover the still glowing coals, I said, "It would be a pity if this beautiful masterpiece of nature were destroyed by my hands through unnecessary carelessness after it has brought such pleasure to my senses and given me a refuge." I guess that she understood, because she did not ask me what I meant.

Three days later, eating a diet of fruit and herbs along the way, we began to follow the road. On the morning after our first day on the road, a helicopter spotted us while we were near the edge of a deep ravine. There was a fast moving river down there. I could hear the rapids below us.

I immediately decided that the two of us must elude my pursuers by going down into the ravine.

As I reached for my hostage to grab her around the waist, she eluded me, picked up a rock and hit me on the head.

After a while, I heard voices. I did not open my eyes in case they were watching me closely. I was lying down. I could feel the metal floor beneath my cheek. My back was up against a seat. I was probably in the helicopter. I had been taken captive.

A wavering voice asked, "You are sure that he is securely bound?"

The steady voice of my former

hostage answered, "Yes. And as an extra precaution, I injected him with a sedative."

A third voice said, "Good. Let's take him back to the research center."

A second later, I heard the start of a motor and a light jerk as the helicopter lifted into the air. Panic seized me!

The muscles of my arms and legs bulged. Adrenalin poured into me from somewhere. It was maybe five seconds before I broke my bonds. I stood up and just barely avoided hitting my head on the ceiling of the helicopter. I lunged forward at the controls and crashed into the wide-eyed and horrified pilot.

In the next second, the helicopter lost all stability and tilted over the edge of the cliff and plunged into the ravine. Down it went and it crashed into the roaring stream. Water rushed into the cabin through the bashed in windows and doors.

I had to get out or the downed helicopter would be my coffin. Half-choking, I made my way through an opening as the helicopter flipped over and over in the current of the river.

Immediately I was met by a swift current of very cold water. It swept me and the battered helicopter down stream. Both the mass of metal and I slammed against the rocks when we were swept over rapids.

Each time as I clawed for a hold, I heard the thundering crash of metal against rock. I clutched and clawed for a hold on each rock I was thrown against. Finally, bleeding and worn, I saw a rock near the shore ahead. With all the rest of my remaining strength, I struggled toward it allowing the torrent to bash me against the rocks that were between me and it.

After extensive maneuvering and more injuries, I was swept against my goal. Mustering all the strength that I could, I pulled myself up on the slippery smooth surface of the rock and out of the water. I lost consciousness.

I am not sure how long I slept before I had the realization that I had to keep moving or I would be captured again. I fought myself awake, forced myself erect, and I began to move downstream, seeking a place to ascend the cliff.

Wait, I thought, above you on this side is the road. You want to ascend the cliff on the other side of the river.

I smiled to myself as I found that my ability to reason was coming back.

As I moved along the sides of the cliff and from rock to rock, I became conscious of the fact that I as I moved, I lost my soreness. Soon, warmth slowly returned to me.

While I journeyed onward, seeking a way to cross, I looked for signs of the remains of the helicopter. Shortly I saw the metallic hulk. It had broken open exposing its contents to the terrible ripping force of the swift stream and the rapids. Upon closer observation, I saw red colored water, an arm, a head, and other body parts caught among the rocks and bobbing up and down with the movement of the flowing stream.

It was the head of my hostage. I shuddered, thinking about that pretty girl and my own near death.

I was soon able to cross the river.

From a summit above the ravine, I stopped to take a last look at the roaring stream below. I thought of that pretty girl broken to pieces and floating in the water. Regret filled my heart. Tears of remorse filled my eyes.

After a few moments pause, I turned my face toward the mountains beyond. I climbed west through the trees with the hope of a new life and freedom in my future.[35]

---

[35] I wrote this story the summer after spending a month in the hospital recovering from encephalitis. That was 1961. I had in mind a series of stories about the central character as he attempted to hide himself in society. Instead, this became the first attempt at a novel that became **Katya and the Solar Wind**. My second attempt at the novel is in this volume and it is entitled: **Surprise! You are a father.** You will find it on page 125.

A THING TO REMEMBER

Once upon a time in the land called Mythology there was an old myth called 'Jupiter'. He was a crafty old man (and dirty too) and thought himself quite the cat's pajamas. He sat himself down upon a stump one day and conceived a thought – it was a happy thought – it was his brainchild. He then went about his duties without much ado and was very pleased with himself and with his fellows and with the world.

But, then, shortly, he began to get headaches. He took aspirin. He drank water. He tried seltzer and decongestant but nothing helped. So, he changed the climate; decreeing that all of the world should be cool and dry; and it was; but that didn't help!

Hera, his wife, was most concerned and so were his friends and all of his many children. They brought seers and physicians and prophets and doctors of philosophy from all over the world. But none seemed able to help.

First the seers predicted that the headaches would end in seven days and seven nights. So all waited patiently seven days and seven nights for the end of the headaches –but they did not end. Matters had become even worse.

Jupiter's head had begun to swell and swell and swell. Indeed, his head was quite swollen.

The physicians decided that it was something he ate – but it couldn't have been. His headaches had been so bad and hurt so much that he ground his teeth and could not eat anything and had not eaten anything for more than seven days and seven nights.

The physicians then decided that it was what he hadn't eaten. So they pried his mouth open with a gold crowbar – for only gold implements were allowed to touch old myths like Jupiter – and they force-fed him for seven days and seven nights. But his headaches did not diminish; and his head continued to swell.

The physicians then decided that his head continued to swell because of bad blood. They bled him; they bled him of his life's blood. – They could do that, you see, because an old myth like Jupiter never dies; he is immortal.

By this time his head was the size of a pumpkin and his body was emaciated by hunger and loss of all blood. He was just skin and bones and head. But the funny thing was that good old Jupiter was enjoying the pain – he had the pained eyes of a mother enduring labor while anticipating the birth of her child.

Jupiter smiled or tried to with his teeth ground together. His smile seemed more like a sneer, but that was not unusual, Jupiter always smiled that way.

The prophets then had their turn. They prayed and offered sacrifices to myths older even than Jupiter – but there was no answer out of the blue; no bolt of lightning to tell them what to do; no voice speaking out of a pillar of fire.

The prophets went away saddened that they could not give their dear old

Jupiter the aid his appearance seemed to require.

Last of all came the doctors of philosophy. They sat before the propped up Jupiter and thought and conversed and thought. Finally they issued their consensus as one: "We have determined that Jupiter is ill – quite ill – but from no observable or actual causes. Jupiter is a hypochondriac. His head swells daily because he is imagining all the ills imaginable and they are piling up in his brain. To drain his brain is not possible for they are imaginary. Jupiter must cure himself." And so they left.

Hera waited and hoped. His friends waited and hoped. His children waited and hoped.

Many months after the beginning of his headaches, Jupiter's head was as big as a Volkswagen Beetle. It was resting in a special crib with his small emaciated body dangling from it like the almost unnoticeable head and legs on a fat and blood engorged tick.

No one was there when it happened except a deaf mute eunuch who was dusting the crib and the cribbed head and motionless torso and arms and legs of Jupiter.

That poor man never heard the gigantic – POP – as Jupiter's head burst like a pimple and he would never have realized anything at all if he had not seen the fully clothed and armored thing rise like ooze from Jupiter's naked brain. (Jupiter was bald).

The frightened man ran quickly away and found Hera and dragged her away from her garden party and into the room where the sick Jupiter lay. When they arrived, all was over. Jupiter was sitting at a table, quite his natural self, and now eating a pomegranate seed.

Hera demanded, "What in god's name have you been doing these past nine months?"

Jupiter, that crafty old boy, gave her something to tickle her innards and later said: "Hera, dear old girl, meet my daughter, Athena."

Athena stepped back into the room from the balcony where she was viewing the world in which she was destined to live as a myth. She was fully seven feet tall and clothed in gold armor; and carrying a gold shield and a gold spear tipped with platinum.

Hera said, "That's a nice name, but what does she do?"

Jupiter laughed and said, "It always takes a woman to think of the practical aspects of creation."

Hera demanded, "Well?"

Jupiter thought a minute and then said, "She is the new goddess of wisdom; armed with the shield of implacable Faith and the spear of Truth to burst the bubbles of falsehood."

And Hera remembered the words of the doctors of philosophy: "Jupiter is a hypochondriac and fills his head with all ills imaginable. You must wait for him to cure himself."

And then Hera smiled.[36]

---

[36] This was written sometime after "Why Is There a Rainbow" which was written in 1965.

A PROBLEM OF VALUE
(A one-act, one-scene play)

(The narrator comes onto the stage to front-center; a spotlight is on him every step of the way. He is wearing a black suit.)

NARRATOR
The curtain will open on a scene familiar during any war.

(The Narrator steps to the right as the curtains open partway, disclosing one side of a trench. It is the evening. Dim ceiling light and dark footlights come on.)

NARRATOR
It is evening. A skirmish of short duration has been over for several hours. The soldiers of one side are now resting by shifts in a protective trench.

(Hank and Chuck are best friends. They

are resting side by side against the earthen wall behind them. Spotlight comes on and pinpoints Hank sitting down and leaning back against the wall with his knees drawn up. His helmet is in place. He is smoking a cigarette. There are a dozen or so cigarette butts lying on the ground in front of him; several are still smoldering.)

NARRATOR
Hank has been chain-smoking for three hours. Chuck has been lying in the same position for as long.

(Another spotlight comes on showing Chuck lying down to the left of the Hank. His hands are folded under the back of his head and his helmet covers his face. His legs are stretched out perpendicular to the wall with one foot on top of the other.)
(Spotlight on NARRATOR goes out; as the spotlights on HANK and CHUCK dim; the ceiling and footlights brighten.)
(Hank lifts the helmet off of his head and lets it fall to the right. The helmet lands

bottom up. Hank uses both hands to wipe the sweat from his forehead and into his hair. His hands gradually move back through his hair as his head bows down. His hands clasp behind his head while his elbows rest on his knees. A cigarette dangles from the corner of his mouth.)

HANK
God, Chuck. What does a guy do?

(Chuck removes his helmet from his face and slowly sits up and moves back toward the wall behind him. He leans his head back against the wall and speaks in even, tired tones.)

CHUCK
Hank, I haven't the slightest idea what you should do. I just choose to forget.

(Hank tosses away his half-finished cigarette and looks up toward heaven with his eyes closed and the muscles of his face and neck tensed.)

                    HANK
     But – God! How can a guy forget?

                    CHUCK
     I suppose one never really does.

(Hank reaches over and pulls a cigar out
of Chuck's shirt pocket. He bites off the
end and jabs the cigar into his mouth.
He stands up, scowling at the world in
general and digs into a front pants
pocket for his lighter. The lighter
doesn't work. Hank tosses it into his
helmet; he holds his left arm out behind
him. Hank doesn't look back as Chuck
places a book of matches into Hank's
open palm. Hank lights the cigar and
puts the book of matches into his own
shirt pocket. Hank exits Stage Right.)

(Chuck slowly resumes the position he
held at the opening of the scene. There
is a period of complete silence before a
short skinny soldier with a thin face
comes onto the stage from the direction
Hank had gone. Percy is doubled over

and clutching his lower abdomen with both hands. Percy moans as he approaches Chuck.)

PERCY

Jesus, Chuck! What the hell is wrong with Hank? That big jackass just kicked me in the balls.

(Chuck removes his helmet and slowly sits up, dragging himself back against the wall again. He leans back for support. He speaks slowly, deliberately, and tiredly – not the yawning type of tiredness.)

CHUCK

Hank wouldn't just kick you in the balls, Percy.

(Percy moans before he speaks.)

PERCY

Well, hell, Chuck! All I said was "I hear you killed five . . . and . . .

(Chuck interrupts Percy and finishes

Percy's sentence.)

CHUCK
And Hank kicked you in the balls.

(Chuck tiredly lies back down and puts his helmet over his face again.)

PERCY (whining)
You goddamned self-centered bastard!

(Percy turns painfully away and walks off STAGE RIGHT. He is still doubled over and clutching his lower abdomen with both hands.)
(There is complete silence for a time. Then a great deal of commotion is heard from backstage from the direction Hank had gone. Several MP's with helmets and rifles cross in front of Chuck from STAGE LEFT. One of them trips over Chuck's feet but catches himself just before falling down.)
(After the MP tripped over Chuck's feet, Chuck takes his helmet off of his face, sits up again, and moves back to lean

against the wall.)
(After another couple of minutes, Percy
returns from STAGE RIGHT; he is so
excited that he has forgotten his recent
injury.)

PERCY
Do you know what that big jackass
did just now?

(Chuck looks disinterestedly at Percy,
but speaks anyway.)

CHUCK
No, what, Percy?

(Percy is buoyant with excitement as he
speaks.)

PERCY
Hank met the C.O. and the C.O. told
Hank that he would get a medal for
his work today. Hank beat the hell
out of him! It took eight guys to
keep Hank from stomping the C.O.'s
guts out! God, those five dead men
really bothered Hank.

(Chuck looks up at Percy and speaks very calmly.)

CHUCK
Percy, Hank stuck three of those five men with his bayonet.

(Percy's face slowly changes from a look of incomprehension to a look of near nausea. He verbalizes with a husky exhalation.)

PERCY
Oh.

(Spotlights come on to shine on both Percy and Chuck as the stage lights dim. These spotlights brighten as the stage lights go out. Percy doesn't move from his position. Chuck slowly lies down again with his legs stretched out with one foot on top of the other and he puts his helmet over his face. A spotlight comes on to pinpoint the NARRATOR where he has been standing as a dark shadow all this while.)

NARRATOR

Why is there a difference between
killing a man with an impersonal
bullet activated by the pull of a
finger on a trigger; and killing a
man, disemboweling a man, ripping
his guts out with the twist of an
impersonal bayonet given force by a
pair of strong arms? Either way
makes a man just as dead. . . .
Is it a problem of value?

(NARRATOR turns his back on the
audience and faces the stage. Percy has
remained immobile all this time, with
widened eyes and stricken face. Percy
has shown more than his profile to the
audience, although he has not looked in
the direction of the audience. The
spotlight on Percy goes out. There is a
short interval before the spotlight on the
NARRATOR goes out.)[37]

---

[37] This was the first part of a three-part term paper written November 13-24, 1964
for Philosophy 201 at Otterbein College.

MY INDIRECT DISCOURSE

Damn it! How many times do I have to tell you, Robinson, that if you had studied for that exam, you would have gotten them all right?

But it was a good program. I had to watch it.

The hell you did. You had your book open and you were ready to study when you heard the television come on. You could have gone down to your room to study, but you didn't. Just think of all the other tests you just got 96% on. How many of those did you study for?

Hardly any, but . . .

I know. Every one of them could have been answered perfectly if you had just taken a little time. What's an hour to you? You haven't anything else to do.

Yes, I do. I . . .

Watch television, read those lousy western novels, think . . .

Sure I think! That's what I am supposed to do isn't it?

Depends on what you think. How many times did you focus on trying to write that book you will never finish? How many times do you . . .

All right! All right! That's enough.

Oh, sure! Now you're going to give me one of those promises again. Well, I've found that you never keep them.

Yes, I do.

When?

Well, remember that time I promised I'd win that Preliminary State Scholarship Test in science?[38]

Sure! But you wanted to win that.

Don't I want to get these tests perfect?

No, you don't.

I don't?

Well, not in the same way at least. On that other test you wanted to make sure nobody surpassed you. So you spent a little time studying for it.

A little time! Why, I . . .

---

[38] These are tests that the State of Ohio was using when I was in high school. If you did well on the Preliminary Test you might choose to take the Final Scholarship test in a subject and be recognized for your academic skill.

It wasn't enough. If you had spent only an hour a day studying, your grade would have been better.

I received an honorable mention, didn't I?

Yes, but that wasn't enough! Now on these other tests you think you can get a better grade than anybody else just because you think you are more intelligent. In a way, I believe you are.

So we're both conceited.

Would you like to shut up and let me finish? . . . Now as I was saying. In a way you are more intelligent, but I have now changed my opinion. You are really quite stupid. Your scholarly opponents are actually more intelligent. They spend from an hour to several hours studying, whereas you may spend only fifteen or twenty minutes. The result is that they get a higher grade than you. I don't like this any more than you do. So, would you care to get busy and work on these subjects?

I can't promise I will, but I will promise to try.

Try hard then. I'm getting a little

tired of not being first. . . . Well, what are you doing just sitting here carrying on a mental conversation with me? . . . Study! All right?

All right![39]

---

[39] I wrote this the spring of 1960. I was in ninth grade. That year I won first place in every subject in the local school. I was quite embarrassed by the attention. After that, I didn't study for any future tests. I simply relied on my memory.

SURPRISE! YOU ARE A FATHER.

As the title suggests, it was a total surprise. My name is Alexander Alexis Dalton and I am fifty-five years old. I have never been married and I was on a mission to Mars for twenty-five years during which time, I became sterile from the constant bombardment of radiation in outer space as well as on the planet Mars itself. Although my hair is white, I have the body of a thirty-five-year-old due to being in zero gravity and the low gravity of Mars for twenty-five years.

I have three Ph.D.'s from M.I.T. so when I retired from the UN Space Service; I was offered a professorship at M.I.T. In addition, I am occasionally consulted as a trouble-shooter or as a detective by various colleagues.

This summer I gave my secretary two months leave of absence with pay. I thought I would take the time to write a novel about my experiences. It turned out that reality was more interesting than the novel I planned to write.

I was sitting at the computer writing my novel when I got an email for an old colleague from years ago at M.I.T. He had been scheduled to go on the mission to Mars with me and ten others, but at the last minute he was offered a grant to do some independent research for the military.

Alex:
   I know you must be very busy with other work, but would you be so kind as to forego your summer plans and help me on a little matter of observation. I have come across a phenomenon that is peculiar and I want to consult with you about it.
   If you are able to come, reply to this email to say so.
   Respectfully yours,
   John Turner

To say the least, I was intrigued. I knew John from our graduate school years together. He was not my favorite person from that time; she had died in a car accident that was never explained.

Nevertheless, I replied that I would be honored to be consulted.

Three days later, a young man with a dark complexion knocked at my door.

He said, "Doctor Dalton?"

"Yes." I answered as I let him into the house.

He asked, "Will you come with me, please."

I said, "Pardon?"

He said, "You are to accompany me, aren't you sir?"

I demanded, "Who are you?"

He didn't answer. Instead, he said, "Doctor Dalton, you sent a message to Doctor Turner three days ago."

I said, "Yes."

He said, "Well, sir, let's go."

I opened my mouth to say something else, but I thought better of it. He waited by the door while I went down the hall to pack my suitcase.

Before returning to the front door, I took my favorite revolver out of the drawer of the night table and slipped it into my shoulder holster.

My visitor held the door open for me

as he motioned to one of his associates to carry my suitcase to a waiting, unmarked car.

We were driven to the center of town where we drove around and switched cars six times in thirty minutes. Eventually we drove to an airport where we boarded a military plane. I had gotten to like my young companion and was pleased when he spoke to me as he escorted me to the passenger section.

He said, "Doctor Dalton, would you give me your autograph? My three sons know all about your time on Mars."

I took a pad of multicolored paper out of my vest pocket. (I always keep a pad handy in preparation for this.) I said, "It's always a pleasure to satisfy children. To whom shall I address it?"

I watched his face as he gave me their names: Alan, Jeff, and Gary. His face brightened the most on that final name.

I asked, "Shall I make out three of them with a short personal message?"

He said, "That would be wonderful, sir."

I said, "There you are," as I handed him the finished autographs. I decided to take the gamble and asked, "May I call you 'Gary'?"

Startled, he leaned closer and whispered, "Sir, I didn't tell you my name." Then having lost his assurance, he asked, "Did I?"

Pleased that I had guessed correctly, I smiled and said, "You didn't, Gary."

He asked, "Then how did you know, sir?"

I didn't respond to his question. Instead, I said, "Gary, call me Alex."

I started to walk away and take my seat.

Gary caught my arm and whispered, "Alex, how did you know my name? It could cost me my job."

I said, "Gary, we are about to take off and it's almost lunch time." I sat down in the next seat over. I said, "Have a seat beside me and be my lunch partner. I'll see if I can explain it to you while we eat."

Aloft, we had lunch together and he

talked about his three boys and his wife; and I talked about the book I was planning to write.

An interesting discussion of Martian politics was interrupted by a colonel who ordered Gary up front.

As Gary left, I asked him, "By the way, Gary, what is your last name?"

"Smith," he replied and began to laugh. He said, "Thank you very much, Alex for everything."

Now Gary knew that I had only guessed his first name. He left; and I knew he would be a friend for life.

The colonel stayed behind. He seemed to have something on his mind but he didn't speak or introduce himself.

I asked, "Well, Colonel?"

The colonel said, "Doctor Dalton, I apologize for the inconvenience we have caused you."

I opened my mouth to say that it was really no trouble, but he was already saying something else.

He said, "We are going to a research outpost in the middle of nowhere. Its location is to give further assurance of its secrecy."

I said, "I gathered that."

He continued, "We are taking all precautions to keep its location unknown to you even after your stay there. You are restricted to this enclosed area where there are no windows, no compasses, or anything else that might hint of our destination." He stopped and looked coldly into my eyes and then he ordered, "Do not try to leave this area! We will use force to keep you here if it is necessary."

As soon as I spoke, I regretted it. I said, "Colonel, I think you are ridiculous."

His neck grew red, but he turned around and walked forward without another word.

I was awakened from a dream about European anteaters when Gary walked down the aisle.

He said, "Alex, we are about to land. Please strap yourself in."

I said, "Under one condition, if you strap yourself into the seat next to me."

He said, "I'd love to, Alex, but I have been ordered not to associate with you." He paused a moment. Then he added, "When I am on duty, that is."

I strapped myself in without any argument.

He said, "Thank you, Alex." Then he leaned closer and whispered, "By the way, my last name is Jeffries. I'll see you sometime after we land." Gary turned and left.

When I stepped off of the plane, I surveyed the landscape. I saw rugged mountains and Rocky Mountain trees.

Well, I decided, I am either in the United States or Canada in the middle of some forest preserve.

A waiting car took me to a hotel-like building where all personnel were housed.

The driver said, "Doctor Dalton, tomorrow morning at ten o'clock, a car will be at your disposal for three hours. You may go anywhere you like, within reason. Your driver may not be permitted to take you to a few certain places. Sometime after lunch, Doctor Turner will receive you. A car will take you to him."

I thanked him; then I went in and got a room.

Although it was only five in the afternoon, I felt very tired and lay down for a short nap before dinner. The next thing I knew, the morning light was shining through my window.

I looked at the clock by the bed. It was five o'clock in the morning. I had slept twelve hours. I shaved, took a shower, and got dressed.

In spite of my hurry, I didn't get down stairs before six. When I got down, I had a little difficulty finding the dining hall.

In the dining hall I saw a pretty brunette sitting alone. Naturally, I seated myself at her table.

I said, "Good morning."

She looked up, smiled, and echoed, "Good morning. Are you new here?" She looked me over. She seemed to be wondering about my young features and white hair.

I admired her features as I said, "Yes, very new. Would you be so kind as to give me your name and your telephone number?"

She giggled and said, "My name is Janet Loughton. And what is your name?"

I held out my hand and said, "I am very pleased to meet you, Janet. I am Alex Dalton."

She shook my hand as she said, "Likewise, Alex." She added, "Now that is a nice, masculine name. Are you named after Alexander the Great?"

We both laughed at the comparison.

I was still holding her hand when I added, "He made a great number of conquests. I'll be satisfied with just one."

She blushed and pulled her hand away as she changed the subject. She said, "We are having ham and eggs for breakfast."

I said, "That sounds good. I am famished."

We were soon served.

In between bites of food, Janet

asked, "Are you any relation to the Dalton that was on a mission to Mars?"

I answered, "Yes, a rather vague relation." Then I asked, "What do you do here?"

She answered, "I am a nurse and a statistician at a research laboratory near here. What do you do?"

I said, "Not much of anything, really. I'm sort of a trouble shooter."

She repeated that phrase as a question, "Trouble shooter?"

I explained, "I am a consultant and sometimes a detective for colleagues."

She commented, "Oh!" Then she asked, "Why are you here?"

I answered, "I don't know yet. Hopefully I will find out soon."

She finished eating and rose to leave. I rose with her and said, "Janet, it was so nice to meet you." And I held out my hand as though to say goodbye.

When she took my hand, I asked, "Janet, will you have dinner with me tonight?"

She answered, "I – I – I guess so."

A messenger came up to us and

said, "Pardon the interruption, Doctor Dalton, but I have a message for you." He held out an envelop to me.

I let go of her hand and took it. The messenger left.

Janet exclaimed, "Doctor Dalton! I am so sorry that I didn't recognize you, sir. Will you please forgive me?"

I asked, "Forgive you for what?"

She answered, "For being so disrespectful, sir."

I held my hand out to her again. She put her hand into mine.

I said, "Janet, you must have dinner with me tonight, please."

She said, "I'll be glad to, sir."

I said, "Janet, my name is Alex."

She murmured, "Thank you very much, Alex." She pulled her hand away and left the dining hall.

I sat down again and opened the envelop and read the message:

Dr. Dalton:

We find that we have made a mistake. Your uncanny powers of observation cause us to revoke the privilege of a car at ten o'clock this morning. But since we do not want you to be bored, we will have our meeting earlier than originally scheduled. The car that was to be at your disposal will bring you to the main laboratory at ten o'clock this morning.

John Turner

Shortly after ten o'clock in the morning, I was driven to a large, low building. Half of it seemed to be underground. It had no protective fence around it. However, it had an unusually wide double door entrance in the middle with an armed guard at each side of the entrance.

I was escorted through a large hall separating the offices from the lab. At each end of the hall there was an exit for emergency use only. An alarm would sound if they were ever opened so they were not guarded.

Once I was in John Turner's office, we went through the usual introductions and greetings.

Then John asked, "Well, Alex, how do you like it?"

I said, "An excellent building, John, but why the large hall."

He said, "It was needed for extra space. At times there is so much information to be catalogued that it is all moved into the hall where I can supervise the process easier."

I asked, "How long have you been working on this experiment?"

He said, "The actual experiment is only nineteen years old. However, I have been working on it for the past thirty years."

I said, "This is the research project that kept you earth side instead of going to Mars with us."

He said, "Yes. It is. This is a very special experiment."

Turner asked the government to sponsor an experiment with human beings. He outlined the whole thing in a proposal and the government jumped at the chance.

A research center was build as far away from the gaping eyes of tourists and the prying eyes of the press as possible. The experiment had to be done in secret.

At the research center, the ovum from a female donor was fertilized with sperm from a male donor in a test-tube to form a zygote. The zygote was caused to divide, forming twins and then triplets and finally quadruplets. It took a while to learn how to do this and end up with four identical fetuses growing in four artificial wombs. Fortunately they had a supply of ova and sperm from the same two donors to do this. Eventually they were successful and had four identical male babies growing in four artificial wombs.

All of the babies did very well for the first three months. An accident took the life of one baby during the fourth month. They lost a second baby during delivery. The two surviving babies were all they had to continue the experiment.

One baby was used as a control and given to human parents to raise. The last baby was put into a fifteen by fifteen cell with machines operated by humans to feed it and clean it.

Both babies were under constant observation. Both ate the best foods and were kept on a similar diet. They were vaccinated at the same time against the same diseases. Both were given the same vitamin supplements in their food.

One had gone to nursery school and kindergarten with other children. Eventually he graduated from high school and was now in college.

The one kept in the fifteen by fifteen cell had never breathed outside air, seen the sunshine, or walked in the rain.

The boy raised by humans with humans was a happy, healthy young man; and thought to be a genius.

The boy raised in isolation by machines was alone and had been alone for nineteen years. No one knew why the boy survived in isolation that long.

Physically, both were alike: six feet six inches tall and weighing two hundred pounds. They both had blonde hair, blue eyes, handsome face, and excellent physique.

The control was a great athlete and was allowed to participate in the safer sports. His observers did not want to take any chances on him becoming disabled by injuries.

The experimental specimen did not learn to walk as soon as the other; once he had, he invented physical exercises that he did in a routine of his own design. He verbalized and made noises and listened for the echo; then he did it again until he tired of the game. He even created his own music by banging on the walls, the floor, and the machines in the room to get different sounds with his hands or with a part of a machine that he dismantled.

I ate lunch with Doctor Turner and a few of his associates in their lunchroom. Halfway through the lunch, we were interrupted by a male nurse.

The nurse said, "Doctor Turner, he is doing it again." Then the man left and headed back to the laboratory.

John Turner said, "Gentlemen, I must leave." He stood up and headed for the door into the hall. Then he turned and said, "Alex, you might as well come with me. This is your problem and you might as well see it now."

My problem! I thought, I wonder what it is.

We hurried out of the staff lunchroom and into the hall. We went down the hall, through a door, and into a laboratory that completely surrounded the specimen chamber or prison where the subject of their experiment was kept.

The outside walls around the prison were filled with observation screens and one entry hatch. The staff could climb above the prison to maintain equipment used in the ceiling inside the prison.

In every view screen I saw a man from all angles. He was completely naked, except for his waist-length hair. He was standing still, leaning slightly forward, with his head tilted to one side as though he were listening for the heavy footfall of an ant.

John said, "See him, Alex. This is your job. You are to decide what he is doing, what he is thinking. He seems to be listening to something, but what? There is nothing for him to hear. Even if he has super sensitive hearing, he will only hear machines in the walls."

At this point, the young man stood up straight and turned his head from side to side as though he heard something moving and wanted to know what it was.

I thought: He has a beautiful body. How did he stay in such good shape in such a tiny prison?

I almost wept when I thought of it. That beautiful boy all alone for nineteen years, how could he stand it?

I caught myself before I wept. I blinked to keep from tearing.

I realized that this prison was all that this boy had every known. He had no choice but to endure it.

John called out, "Alex, did you hear me?"

John knew full well that I am easily drawn away from the subject at hand if I find something more interesting.

I answered, "Yes, John, I heard you.

You want me to tell you why he does what he does."

John said, "That's right! This is the shortest time that he has ever done what you saw him do. Once he held that position for two hours. Two hours!"

I asked, "When did this begin?"

John answered, "Three weeks ago."

I puzzled for a moment.

Then I asked, "May I have his complete history?"

John said, "Yes. I will give you the last three years."

I said, "John, I want everything from the beginning until now."

John said, "All right, I'll have a car take them to your room. But really, I don't see the need for that. There is so much to read and so little time."

I echoed, "So little time?"

He said, "Yes."

I asked, "Why?"

After my question, he was silent for a moment; and then he continued with an explanation. "I am due to make a report on my findings to a delegation of scientists and government officials. I don't want to make anything known until I am absolutely certain that this latest development has no significance at all."

I said, "I see. Well, don't worry. I will read it tonight and observe him tomorrow."

He was relieved and said, "Thank you, Alex."

I left in the car with the history in the trunk. The driver helped me carry the boxes of duplicate files up to my room; then he left.

I read the first fourteen years before dinner.

Turner's guinea pig had laughed, gurgled, and played like a normal child. When he cried, he was fed; when he needed to be cleaned, he was cleaned; all by machines. He learned early that to deposit his waste products in a fast moving, artificial stream flowing through one corner of his cell was necessary for his comfort. He learned to get his food from a machine and drink water from a fountain. His whole life was routine.

There was light for the same

amount of time that there was dark. At night, water fell in a torrent from the ceiling for a full ten minutes in a simulated cloud burst, intending to cleanse everything. He slept in one corner of his cell on a raised platform that was kept at a higher temperature then the rest of the cell.

He had talked to himself in a language only he could understand. He had gone over every inch of his cell and seemed to memorize each crevice and bump. He dismantled the mechanical arms that hung from the ceiling over his bed and put them back together again a number of times.

He was very adventurous; and one day, lost two nuts from the arms in the stream and never found them again. He had counted, or, rather, seemed to count. He held up his fingers and toes as if he were adding them together; and then, he took them away as if he were subtracting. There were many more interesting observations.

I noticed the time. I hurried to wash and change and go down to dinner. I found Janet waiting for me.

I said, "I'm terribly sorry, Janet, that you had to wait for me. Will you forgive me?"

She laughed and said, "You are forgiven, Alex."

I said, "That's a relief. I would hate to have you angry with me."

She smiled and asked, "How many girls have fallen for your lines?"

I smiled and watched her face. Slowly the hint of a blush shone on her cheeks, but she steadily returned my gaze.

I broke the moment by sitting down. I asked, "How long have you worked here, Janet?"

She answered, "Three years."

I asked, "How do you send letters home, if you don't know where you are?"

Thoughtfully she looked down at the ice in her glass of water; and then she spoke very slowly, "If I wanted to send any letters, or if I got any letters, they would be postmarked: Washington, D.C. An airplane comes once a month with mail addressed to anyone of us in care of Special Research, Washington, D.C. The letters going out have that same return address."

Dinner was served and we ate in silence for ten minutes or so.

Breaking the silence, I asked, "Janet, what do you think of Doctor Turner's experiment."

She whispered intensely, "I think it stinks. That boy hasn't had any love, any friends, or any life! I think it's rotten to treat a human being that way!"

We finished eating in silence. After dinner, there was a movie and we went to it. We sat together in the plush seats and I held her hand. After a while, she leaned her head against my shoulder and I put that arm around her. I think she fell asleep.

We had a night-cap before I walked her to her room.

At her door, I said good night.

She responded, "Good night, Alex." Then she unlocked her door and began to step inside.

On impulse, I called, "Wait a

minute, Janet."

She turned and opened her mouth to speak. Opportunity there, I encircled her waist in an embrace and kissed her.

For a moment she responded to my kiss. Then she squirmed out of my arms and pushed me away. She exclaimed, "Doctor Dalton!" - With mock horror in her voice and an impish look on her face.

I gave her a look and she knew what was on my mind; and I whispered, "Janet?" - Hinting with my voice that I would be very good to her. I wanted to say more, but she backed into her room keeping eye contact with me all the time with a smile on her face and shaking her head no at the same time.

As she closed the door in my face, she whispered, "Good night, Alex."

I stood staring at the door that had just closed and then I whispered, "Good night, Janet. I had hoped for more."

Then I went back to my room and finished my reading.

The boy had always been energetic.

He had been doing cartwheels and somersaults at an early age. In his fifteenth year, he seemed to take a more serious outlook on his physical fitness. He began to invent various exercises that stretched and strengthened his muscles. He seemed to have a sense of music and rhythm, for he often did exercises as though he were performing ballet.

He spent hours at a time doing physical exercises; his physical condition for one cramped in a cell with a floor area less than two hundred and twenty-five square feet, was superb.

I went to sleep thinking of what he might have been thinking while he was standing still earlier that day. In my memory, I went through his whole life, beginning with what might have been his earliest recollection. Both my conscious and my sub-conscious minds were occupied with the problem; and I dreamed that I was him.

There is something else! I can sense it! That last time I went to sleep,

I sensed, as on other occasions that I wasn't alone in my cell.

I must check the walls again! I went from wall to wall feeling every inch. I came to the spot where there were the most bumps and crevices. I went over the spot several times as I had always done.

It was changed! It wasn't the same! Something was different!

A cold fear enveloped my heart as I checked the present wall with the one in my memory.

They were different! The bumps and crevices were rearranged!

Then I felt it. Cold air flowing from a pin-sized source blew against the hair on my arm.

Stone-faced, I went to check the remaining wall, the floor, and the ceiling to see if there were anymore changes. There were no others.

I decided to double check my findings. I went over the whole surface again and found the same results.

My world was changed! It had never changed on its own before. I had caused the only change that had occurred before. I had lost a nut from each of the mechanical arms that hung from the ceiling.

I went to the arms and took them apart again. I laid them out on the floor and then put them back together again. The same two nuts were still missing. I had made the change in the arms; I had not changed the wall!

That night I was wakened by a sound that I had never heard before – an intimate sound, like the ones the arms had made when they had been working. I sat up and listened until the sound stopped.

The next day, I heard more sounds that were extraordinary to me. I began to think. I thought much deeper than I had thought before.

Now, I said to myself, if I am the only one that can change things; and things that make sounds like those the arms made cannot change things, then how did the wall change if I didn't do it?

The wall cannot change itself, for it doesn't have arms; and the arms that hang from the ceiling above me cannot reach the wall to be the cause of the change. I have arms, and I can move from one place to another. Therefore, I could have made the change, but I didn't do it! That means that there must be something else that can make changes like I can! Why haven't I seen it? Maybe it doesn't want to be seen?

But I want to see it! How can I see it if it doesn't want to be seen? What would happen if I didn't get up to eat breakfast, didn't get up to eat lunch, didn't get up to eat supper, didn't move at all? Should I try it? I need to practice first. I began to practice.

I stopped to listen and didn't move a muscle while I listened. I sat on the floor to think and didn't move a muscle while I thought. I am ready to escape!

I woke up out of a deep sleep. I sat up in bed and yelled, "Escape! Escape! "

My breathing was swift and short. I was wet and hot from sweat.

Escape! I thought urgently, I must warn them!

Wait, I cautioned myself, am I a scientist? Of course I am. So why not see if the boy can escape.

I whispered aloud, "Yes, that is just what I will do."

I shaved, showered, and dressed.

Janet wasn't there when I went to eat breakfast.

I must be early, I decided.

Say, what time is it? I looked at my watch. Ten o'clock already?

I had overslept.

I ate breakfast hurriedly and called for a car.

I got to the main lab and nodded at the two guards at entrance. They let me pass. I found the hall deserted. I went down to Turner's office and found the door unlocked and no one inside.

I was about to leave when I noticed my name on a folder on his desk. I opened it. It was my medical history.

He was probably checking up on me, but why would he do that?

I leafed through it. It went all the

way back to my great grandfathers and great grandmothers.

I wasn't interested. I started to put the folder back where I got it when I saw another folder that had been under the one in my hand.

It belonged to Mary Sue Johnson. She had been my fiancée but she was killed in an unexplained auto accident over thirty years ago. Why did he have her medical history?

Now I was perplexed. I picked up her file. Underneath it were two DNA charts: one for me and one for Mary Sue. I saw my dominants and my recessives; and Mary Sue's dominants and recessives.

And beneath them was a third DNA chart for a boy: blonde hair; blue eyes; and high intelligence. His height had come from Mary Sue's DNA.

Oh, my God, I thought.

I sat down in Turner's desk chair. He had used my sperm and Mary Sue's ova in his experiments. We had left sperm and ova samples in storage on earth when we were accepted for the

Mars program. John Turner had taken those samples and used them. All of the zygotes and all of the babies he had created for his experiments had been our children. We never gave him our permission for him to use our sperm and ova samples.

I could sue John Turner and the government.

I laughed. It was more of a sob than a laugh. Tears were flowing down my cheeks.

I was very careful to wipe off any fingerprints that I left on the files and DNA charts as I put them back where I found them.

I had permission to be here or the guards would not have let me into the building. I checked the revolver in my shoulder holster. It was loaded. I knew it was, but I checked it anyway. I put it back and wiped the tears from my eyes with my fingertips.

I left his office and went down the hall to the laboratory. When I went through the door, John noticed me.

He called, "Alex, look at this!"

I saw the blonde giant that I had seen before on the view screens. Now I saw him as our son.

I could have killed John Turner right then and there, but I didn't. I squelched my rage and tried to appear as calm as possible.

I did not let my emotion show as I said, "So?"

Turner said, "He's been like that for hours!"

Then I realized what I was to have seen. The boy was not moving. He was lying on his platform bed and he was completely motionless. I couldn't even see him breathing.

I asked, "Is he alive?"

Turner nodded his head and then he said, "Yes, he is. His breathing is so slow that it is hardly picked up by the electronic ears. His heart-beat cannot be found! What do you think about that?"

I said, "I don't know, John. This is quite different than standing still and listening." I didn't offer more than that.

The man studying the psychological

effects of the experiment on the subject said, "It's just what I've been telling all of you. The long seclusion has finally broken down his resistance to insanity. This is the final stage. He has gone into a coma."

Turner said, "It might not be a coma. He may just have overslept."

Everyone except me had a nervous laugh at that.

Then Turner said, "Check everything. Then go back and check it again. He may have contracted a disease. The exhaust fans may not be working properly. He may have hit his head on something."

As an afterthought, he asked, "What about his temperature?"

Janet called out, "Ninety eight point two degrees."

I hadn't even noticed that she was in the lab. Now I saw her in her white uniform. She was standing in front of a view screen and monitoring the subject's vitals.

After she spoke, she turned around and saw me looking at her. We made eye contact across the room

I heard John curse and then he said, "Now that just isn't enough to warrant immobility! He may just be thinking, meditating or whatever he's done before."

No one agreed or negated. All the other people in the laboratory just stood there looking at their boss.

Janet was still looking into my eyes. She licked her lips and then swallowed as she blushed. And then she turned away from me to look at the view screen behind her.

John Turner roared, "Well, what the hell are you waiting for! Get busy!"

It took two hours for the staff to check everything. After all the reports were in, John Turner sat hunched over in a chair for ten minutes without saying anything. He tapped his fingers on a table top all that time. Finally he broke the silence and said, "He hasn't moved yet, has he."

One of his subordinates said, "Sir, he hasn't moved for eight hours."

John turned to the fellow and said, "Do you think I'm stupid?" To the rest of the staff he said, "All right. The robot arms won't work because he broke them. We have to check him manually; so we will put him to sleep. Somebody give him some gas!"

Several people went to do the task. Turner and a few others went to get ready to enter the cell.   Janet was among them. She was in charge of the subject's vitals. The rest of us gathered around the view screens to watch.

After the customary time for the anesthetic to work, Turner and his usual chosen few went through the hatch and into the prisoner's cell. They were wearing hoods, face masks, gloves, and scrubs with booties over their shoes.

In the excitement of the moment, no one was there to close the hatch after them. The group drew near their naked subject lying unmoving on his bed.

Someone yelled, "Hey! Somebody! Close the hatch!"

One of them turned back to do that.

At that moment, the blonde-giant

came alive. He saw the open hatch and a bunch of face-less menacing monsters dressed in white coming toward him.

The young titan ran through the group of menacing figures nearby and toward the hatch. He grabbed the one solitary figure in front of the hatch and carried it with him out of his prison.

In the laboratory, everyone was stunned at the sight of their prisoner out of his cell. I could have reacted, but I had already decided to be an observer during his attempt to escape

At that moment one of the staff came into the lab from the hallway after a bathroom break.

The young giant ran to the open door and knocked that person out of his way. We could hear him racing down the hallway until the door closed behind him.

All of this happened in less than a heartbeat. At the same time I heard someone behind me say, "He's got Janet!"

Now I reacted faster than anyone else. I ran to the door used by my son, opened it, and ran down the hallway after him. He carried Janet clutched against his chest with his arms wrapped around her back.

I accelerated into a sprint and I tackled him in front of the emergency exit door at that end of the hall. He went down to his knees with me holding onto his ankles.

Now the boy was terrified. He got to his feet with me holding onto him and dragged me to the emergency door.

The exit door looked different from anything he had ever seen. It was attractive. It had a lighted exit sign above it. It had a window above a bar that stuck out into the hall.

He banged Janet's buttocks against the crash bar and the door opened. My head and knees caught against each side of the doorway and I did not have the strength to hold him there. He got away.

Alarms were now sounding in the building and all over the compound.

Someone helped me up and we all ran out of the emergency exit. We were just in time to see the guards usually posted at the front door rushing toward us.

We looked up the mountain behind the laboratory building and saw the young titan running up the mountain with Janet slung over his shoulder like a rag doll.

As all of the others, I watched him racing through trees, around boulders, over the mountain top, and out of sight.

Now an uproar burst out; everyone talking at once, blaming, rationalizing, and marveling.

I was still staring at the point where my son had disappeared carrying Janet when someone put his hand on my shoulder.

I turned to face whoever it was. It was John Turner. Between gritted teeth, I said, "John, I could kill you. How could you do this to my son, to Mary Sue's son? You dated Mary Sue in college. You even asked her to marry you. How could you do what you did to the child of someone you loved?"

He answered, "Someone I didn't love anymore." Then he said, "You read the files on my desk. I knew I should have put them away before I went to the lab."

I said, "You were going to tell me anyway. That's why you brought me here."

He said, "Yes, but I did not plan to tell you that Mary Sue was the mother."

I wanted to hit him in his smug face. He had no remorse. He even seemed pleased with himself.

Suddenly I felt the weight of the gun in my shoulder holster. I wanted to pull the gun and shoot him dead. Instead, I ground my teeth together and turned away. I looked up the mountain where my son ran. I knew exactly which pair of trees he ran between last.

After a moment, I asked, "What efforts are being made to find them?"

Then I turned to look at Turner. He had stepped back out of my reach. I saw that the two guards were coming toward me with their guns out.

When I didn't move, John raised his hand and the two guards stopped moving and stood still. They didn't put their guns away, but they stood there watching me.

I asked, "Is anyone looking for them?"

He said, "A ground search party will leave shortly. I don't expect any results from that because it will be dark very soon. We could search from the air, but our only helicopter is in a hanger out of commission. I ordered it to be repaired immediately. It will be ready to fly by morning. It will be easier to find them in the daylight."

We looked at each other. Some of the animosity we had felt toward each other after Mary Sue became my fiancée was showing. We stood looking at each other for a couple of minutes.

I broke the silence. I asked, "John, did you have Mary Sue killed so you could use the ova she had in storage?"

She had died shortly after he got the research grant and had dropped out of the Mars program.

He answered, "God no. Her death was simply a happy circumstance."

That was a mixed message if I ever heard one.

I said, "I'm going back to my room and dress for mountain climbing. Then I am going with your search party. I don't trust you and I don't trust them."

He gestured with his head toward the armed guards behind him and said, "I could have you arrested or killed."

I said, "John, you have got a lot of guilt on your conscience or you would never have sent me that note. You wanted me here so you can release my son into my custody."

He nodded and said, "That's right. It was either that or euthanize him; time is up; the research project is over."

At that moment, I saw a search party heading up the mountain after the escaped prisoner. All five members of the party carried a tranquilizer gun. Gary Jeffries was in the lead.

I didn't bother changing my clothes. I followed them.

I caught up with them on the other side of the mountain. They were standing in a little meadow trying to decide which direction the escapee had gone. There was no trail. In the dark, they couldn't see any footprints or any other sign of him and his hostage.

By the time I reached the group of five men, four of them walked past me on their way back over the top and on down the mountain to the compound.

Gary said, "Hi, Alex. I thought I would wait for you."

We shook hands.

Gary said, "I heard a rumor that you are the father of the prisoner who escaped. Is that true?"

I said, "I didn't know that until just before he escaped. How did you hear about it?"

Gary said, "Your conversation with Doctor Turner was overheard. Everyone has heard about it by now."

I asked, "Do you know anything about these mountains?"

He said, "I've been up here hunting a couple of times over the years. If he kept moving in the same direction, he would come to a river gorge in about fifteen miles. It is too dark to see now. We might as well go back and get a goodnight's sleep before using the helicopter in the morning."

Going back was easier. There was twilight on that side of the mountain.

I awoke before sunrise the next morning, an eager and determined man. As I dressed, I left my gun behind. I didn't want to be tempted to use it. After breakfast, I went to the hanger where the copter was to have been overhauled.

Gary informed me that Colonel Banes and three other men had taken the copter two hours before my arrival. They went with the explicit intent of finding and killing the escapee.

I said, "They can't do that, Gary. He is a human being. He is naked and unarmed. He isn't a danger to anybody."

Gary said, "I am sorry Alex, but they seem to think that he is. The Colonel says that he fractured a man's skull when he made his escape."

I said, "If that happened, it was accidental. Something like that can happen in a football game. They don't punish players for doing that."

Gary said, "I agree, Alex; but you can't tell the Colonel that. He has made up his mind."

I said, "Janet Loughton is with him. Maybe they won't be able to kill him while she is with him. She would be a witness to it; unless they kill her too."

We sat down on a bench and waited for the helicopter to return.

Doctor John Turner joined us in fifteen minutes. We told him what had happened.

John said, "Oh, hell. I am sorry Alex, but Colonel Banes is the only one who outranks me on this compound."

That gave me an idea and I made my plans while the three of us waited for the helicopter to return.

Three hours later, it returned; and I thanked God that it was only for gas.

We went to talk to the Colonel while the helicopter was being refueled.

John said, "Colonel Banes, sir, I would like to have the use of the helicopter now."

The Colonel said, "So you can look

for your pet and bring him back alive? No way. I want him dead. He is no longer of any use to us."

I said, "Look, here, Colonel, there is no cause for that."

The Colonel said, "No cause! That monster killed one of my men!"

Gary said, "Sir, he didn't kill that man; he just put him in the hospital with a concussion; and right now, the injured man is in satisfactory condition."

The Colonel raged, "You call a fractured skull a "satisfactory' condition? That animal has no right to live!"

I said, "Colonel, he is not an animal. He is a man."

The Colonel glared at me and said, "Can you call that thing a man after he has been locked up in isolation for twenty years?"

I saw that it was useless to talk to him.

The helicopter was refueled and ready to leave again. The pilot and two other men were already inside it. The Colonel headed for it.

I called, "Colonel!"

The Colonel turned around to face me and I hit him on the side of the head as hard as I could. He went down. He was unconscious.

I called out, "Doctor Turner, will you take charge?"

With a broad grin on his face, he said, "Certainly." Then to the Colonel's three men in the helicopter he said, "Gentlemen, would you be kind enough to carry your Colonel to the hospital and leave the helicopter for us?"

They looked at each other. They knew who was second in command. They said, "Yes, sir."

They got out of the helicopter and carried the Colonel away.

Gary got into the pilot's seat and started the engine. I got in beside Gary and John got in the back behind me.

Aloft, we flew to the main lab, and from there, we followed the path my son had taken.

I said, "He would run in a straight line until he came to an obstacle that he could not go over or around."

Gary said, "Well, this is the direction

that he went. And there is the first obstacle that he could not go over or around. We are fifteen miles from the compound."

It was the river gorge.

I looked down as we hovered over the area. There was a recent landslide not far from the direct line that my son may have taken.

Now that I had a landmark, I said, "Set the copter down, Gary. Let's have a look around."

Gary found a burned out area above the gorge not far away. He set down there.

I got out of the helicopter and headed for the landslide area. I had plotted a course while we were aloft and knew how to get there.

John and Gary followed me.

I went to the edge of the cliff that had been in a straight line from the compound. Below was the river. I could hear the river as it crashed over the rapids.

I looked for a way down. There was a ledge below that may have been a step down to the bottom of the gorge.

I said to the two men behind me, "Do you know what I would have done? I would not have turned to the right or to the left and I would not have jumped into the gorge. I would have looked for a way down. It would have gotten me as far away as possible from the compound, as the crow flies."

I turned to Gary and said, "Gary, the helicopter has an infrared detector doesn't it?"

Gary said, "Yes it has."

I said, "I'll bet the Colonel used it as they flew in either direction along the top of the gorge. He would have been looking for body heat.

"I think my son would go down to the river and try to lose himself; just like he lost the nuts for the mechanical arms in the water in his prison.

"John, you and Gary walk along the edge of the cliff and see if there is any easier way to get down then right here."

They headed out. John went north and Gary walked south.

I took off my shoes and socks and

stripped to my underwear. Then I went over the edge of the cliff to the shelf that I saw from above. I saw a bloody footprint. Then I saw another one.

I used the same hand and footholds that my son would have used. He was six foot six; I was only five foot eleven. It was hard for me to reach some of the hand and footholds, but my son had been carrying Janet over his shoulder.

John Turner was the first one to notice that I was no longer standing at the edge of the cliff. He yelled for Gary. Soon the two men were above me, looking down.

John yelled, "You stupid fool. You'll kill yourself!"

I didn't answer. I concentrated on continuing my descent.

I heard Gary call, "Come on, John, we'll take the helicopter down."

It would take some time for them to walk up the mountain to the helicopter.

I hoped they didn't try to come into the gorge while I was still climbing down. The turbulence from the blades could cause me to fall to my death or to terrible injury.

I didn't hear the engine start. I was too busy. I was stretched out full-length searching for toe-holds with my bare feet.

I was at the bottom of the gorge before Gary attempted to bring the helicopter into the gorge. I was thankful for that.

I heard the whirr of the helicopter above my head. I looked up.

It came down slowly; then it was jostled by the turbulence of the air bouncing against the sides of the gorge. It would have been too dangerous to attempt a landing. Gary took the helicopter out of the gorge.

I didn't hear it land. I didn't hear the engine shut off. The roar of the rapids was in my ears.

I gazed along the base of the cliff. I guessed that they would be in a cave. It would be the logical hiding place. No one could see into a cave from above. But he would not know about caves; he would have to walk into one out of curiosity or by accident. So I looked for footprints on the ground around me.

I saw one bloody footprint, but it didn't tell me which way he went, upstream or down stream. He might even have walked into the water. There wouldn't be any footprints in the water.

I decided to go down stream. My son had lost the two nuts for the mechanical arms in the water. They would have disappeared in the direction of the water's flow.

I walked along the shore looking for a cave or other hiding place. I checked every crevice and cavity I passed. I had walked about a mile downstream before I saw it. There was a dark shadow at the base of the cliff two hundred feet further downstream. I raced toward it. It was the entrance to a cave.

I slowed down at the entrance and proceeded with caution. I would need surprise on my side if I were to overcome the young titan.

He didn't know that I was his father. And if he ever found out and learned what a father was, he might hate me for what had been done to him.

It was thoughts like these that brought tears to my eyes and made it harder to see in the interior of the cave.

I crept stealthily and slowly; waiting for my eyes to stop tearing and to adjust to the darkness.

The smaller entrance to the cave began to open up into a larger chamber. I huddled against a wall and pressed myself to the floor as I crept along. The cavern was about twenty feet in diameter. Just about the size of the prison that he left. It was roughly the shape of a hemisphere. That made the ceiling five feet higher than his prison.

I continued to creep forward until I could see the whole of the interior. To one side there was a white figure leaning over a larger, darker hulk. I stood up; ready for anything.

The white figure turned toward me and said, "Alex!"

I said, "Janet!"

She was in my arms in a moment. She was naked except for her bra and panties.

She began to cry and I kissed away

each tear.

When she stopped crying, I asked, "Are you all right?"

She said, "I'm fine, Alex; but I think the boy has pneumonia."

She pulled out of my arms and walked back to the darker figure lying on the ground.

I followed. As I drew nearer, I recognized Janet's clothes. They covered the hulk. They weren't white anymore. They were stained by the green of the shrubbery that he ran through and the earth from the cliff as he climbed down with Janet over his shoulder.

I bent over my son and moved Janet's clothing away from his body. I pressed my ear to his chest and listened. I could hear his labored breathing. His lungs was filling up with fluid.

His skin was warm to my ear. I put my hand on his forehead. He was warm there as well.

I said, "I think it is pneumonia. Running naked up the mountain with you over his shoulder was too much for him. He got overheated and then chilled."

I knelt and pulled his waist length hair up from under the clothing and laid it out behind his head and away from his body; it was full of his sweat. Then I moved the clothing back to cover him from the chill in the cave.

Some of his hair covered the features of his face. I gently brushed it out of the way.

I said, "Look at his face, Janet. What do you see?"

She came over and knelt beside me and looked at the boy's features.

Kneeling side by side, we must have been a sight: the two of us naked to our underwear.

As she looked at the boy's face, she saw my forehead, my nose, and in spite of the scraggly beard, my chin.

It dawned on her and she turned to look me in the eye. She said, "Oh my God! Are you his father?"

There was a look of horror in her face. She seemed about to pull away from me. I grabbed her and held on to her. We were chest to chest and I had pinned her arms to her sides so she couldn't hit me.

I said, "Calm down. I didn't know that I was his father until yesterday."

Then I began to weep. I wept so hard I couldn't hold onto her anymore. I expected her to hit me or, at least, move away from me. She didn't. She pulled my head down to her breasts and rocked with me as I cried.

When I had cried it out, I sat up a little. She let me move but continued to keep her arms around my neck. Then she kissed me as I had kissed her earlier.

She kissed away every tear. Then she kissed me on the mouth with so much passion.

When we came up for air, she whispered into my ear, "I wish I had brought you into my room after we had dinner together the other night. I have wanted you so much since then. You made me wet thinking about you when you came into the laboratory and looked at me."

I laughed and said, "Then all of this

happened."

She laughed with me.

I kissed her again and said, "We need to get my son to safety, then maybe we can spend some quality time together."

She said,"Oh, Alex, you should have seen him after he found this cave. He set me down so gently. I had lost my face mask when he ran through the woods and the hood was pulled back from my hair. I wish you could have seen the awe and wonder on his face when I sat up and looked at him. I was the first human face he had ever seen, except his own reflection. He was like a child seeing a puppy for the first time. His eyes glowed as I smiled and spoke softly to him. He was very tired and went to sleep with his head on my lap. So much like a child."

She reached around me and put her hand in the boy's hair and caressed him on his temple. She said, "How is it possible that you did not know that he existed until yesterday?"

I told her about John Turner and his

grant to do research for the military. I told her about Mary Sue Johnson, my fiancée. I told her about getting the letter from Turner and coming to the compound and discovering the truth.

She was silent while she thought about what I had told her; and then she said, "Alex, I know what we were supposed to do if he ever escaped. We were to tranquilize him and then put him back in his cell. But I wonder if that would even work. He has been outside; he has seen another human being. He would never be happy locked away in isolation again."

I said, "John told me that the experiment was over and test subject in isolation was to be terminated; however, he felt so guilty about what he has done that he wanted me to take custody of my son."

Janet said, "Wow. He is going against military procedure. How does he expect to get away with it?"

I said, "That's why he brought me into it. He hopes my fame and stature with the scientific community will enable me to take custody of my son and they won't be able to object."

Janet said, "I hope he is right."

I kissed her again.

She was panting by the time we broke our kiss. She said, "I want you so badly, but we have a sick child to care for."

I adjusted the erection I had in my jockey shorts.

She noticed and laughed at me.

I said, "I'd better go out and see if I can find Gary and John."

She asked, "Gary Jeffries and John Turner are with you?"

Now I explained how I had found her and who had come with me.

Just as I was about to leave her, Gary found his way into the cave. He stood still as his eyes adjusted to the darkness, then he came forward.

He looked at me and then he looked at Janet. Her nipples were erect and prominent in her bra; her panties were clinging to her vulva.

Still looking at Janet, he said, "Alex I was worried. I am sure glad I found you." Then he said, "Janet, you are one very beautiful and sexy woman."

She blushed all the way down to her bra.

Ignoring what Gary said about Janet, I said, "Gary, how did you get down here."

Still looking at Janet, Gary said, "Rope."

I knew that John Turner could not pilot a helicopter and he would not have been able to come down a rope into the gorge.

I said, "Gary, climb back up the rope. Take the rope back to the helicopter; fasten the harness to the rope and then drop it down from the helicopter with the hoist. That way you won't have to bring the helicopter into the gorge. John can help you."

Gary said, "Yes, that would work!"

Gary was still looking at Janet with something in his eyes that Janet did not like.

She covered the crotch of her panties with her hands and said, "Gary, I ought to slap you. What if I told your wife about this?"

Gary didn't say anything as he backed away from Janet. Finally, he turned around and left the cave.

It would be a half hour or more before we would need to be out of the cave. I went to Janet and put my left hand around her back and my right hand over her hands where they covered her crotch; and I kissed her.

It wasn't long before we made love on top of my undershirt and jockey shorts. Janet came many times and I came once in twenty minutes. Then we got back into our underclothes before we hauled my son out of the cave.

It was another fifteen minutes before the helicopter hovered over the gorge. We saw John leaning out of one side of the helicopter. He was ready to help anyone in the harness get inside when the hoist pulled them up.

We saw Gary lean out the window on the pilot's side. He dropped his shirt out of the window and waved.

I caught it and handed it to Janet. She put it on and buttoned it up. It covered her bra and her panties like a nightie.

She came over and kissed me and whispered, "I'll have to thank Gary for this. Having him gawk at me is one thing; having John Turner gawk at me is another."

I whispered, "Just be careful how you thank him."

She gave me a playful slap and whispered, "I'll get you for that."

I whispered back, "I hope you do." And then I kissed her again.

The harness was down. I found my outer clothes hanging from it. I pulled them loose and put them with Janet's clothes.

I helped Janet get into the harness. She would go up first so she could help John get my son out of the harness and into the helicopter.

I put all of her clothes and my outer clothes into her arms so they could be used to cover my son once he was in the helicopter. I wasn't sure what kind of rescue equipment was in the helicopter.

I watched Janet ascend. As she began to sway a little, she closed her eyes. John got her into the helicopter and soon the harness came down again.

I had John lower the harness until I could get my son into it without having to lift him off of the ground. Then I waved okay and watched him ascend.

It took a while for them to get him into the helicopter harness and all. It took a little longer before the harness came down for me.

When I got into the helicopter, John took the co-pilot's seat. I closed the door and looked down on the floor. Janet was sitting there with my son's head in her lap. He was lying there in fetal position with our clothes covering his body. She was caressing him and kissing him as she sang a lullaby.

I got out of the harness and put it away. Then I sat down with her and held her and my son on my lap.

John said, "The Colonel ordered Gary to fly back to the compound. I ordered Gary to go directly to the nearest civilian hospital. That's where we are headed. We also got orders to land at a nearby air force base. I ordered Gary to ignore those orders as well. I could get in a lot of trouble for that. But once the news gets out about your son, I will be drummed out of the scientific community anyway."

I said, "John, I don't want the publicity. I don't want my son or any of us hounded by reporters or government agents for the rest of our lives. The military doesn't want anyone to know about this experiment. Why don't we all keep quiet and not say anything about this at all."

Gary and John promised to keep the whole thing a secret. Everyone else at the research compound had taken a vow of secrecy before coming to the compound in the first place.

John wouldn't get the credit for what he had learned through his experiment, but he wouldn't be castigated for doing it either. He felt so guilty about it that he was happy to accept this solution to the problem.

When we got to the civilian hospital, I had my son put into a private room with security guards at the door. I used my unlimited credit card to pay for that.

Janet and I stayed in the room with him. A doctor came and authorized a sedative and an antibiotic put into a drip. Janet as a nurse would oversee his instructions.

Using my unlimited credit card, Janet and I bought a thirty-acre estate with a privacy fence around the main house and grounds. Once my son was out of any danger, we kept him sedated until we could haul him by ambulance to a private jet; fly him to the closest airport to our new home; and haul him by ambulance to the estate.

Slowly, over time, we helped our son learn to speak and to read and to trust us as parents. The trust took a long time.

We call our son Andrew. He can use the bathroom by himself, although he doesn't like toilet paper; he prefers the bidet.

He calls us Mom and Dad, but

doesn't really understand the full meaning of those words.

I have no idea where my other son is. John Turner would not divulge that. He did not want anyone to know about that part of his experiment either.

John assures us, when he visits, that our other son has loving parents and is embarked on a wonderful career in science.

We are expecting an additional member of the family in six months. Now that is another story, how Janet finally got pregnant by me. She refused artificial insemination by a donor. She wanted to give birth to my child.

After much research, John was able to find one of my sperm samples left on earth before the Mars expedition. Janet was delighted to put it to use.

I am satisfied with the first fifty-five years of my life. I expect the next fifty or so to be even better than the first.[40]

---

[40] This is the second story I wrote about this theme of being a lab experiment. I wrote this in 1963 while I was at Otterbein College.

Dear Reader,

ODDS AND ENDS: Stories and Essays From the Sixties is a collection of thirty essays or stories written between 1959 and 1969. One or more could be labeled: Science fiction, Fantasy, Horror, Romance, or Satire. They were written while the author was in high school and college in the sixties. They have never been published before. They are in the order for the best read. However, you can read them in any order that you choose. I hope you will enjoy reading them.

In 2013, I began to e-publish. I wrote **Summer** in 1998, but I published it first because it is dedicated to my wife, Carolyn, the love of my life. It is about pain and suffering and the difficult choices people face, and how love can overcome anything. It is a book for adult readers.

When the Dew Fell on the Okra is my first children's book to be published. It was written in December 1966. When I graduated from Otterbein College in January 1967, I gave it to people who had been a help to me. Thanks to Rebecca Swift, my illustrator, it is now available for you to give to someone you care about.

LIGHT AND TENDER BLUE and Other Stories from the Sixties is a collection of fourteen short stories or novelettes written between 1960 and 1964. One or more can be labeled: Science fiction, Fantasy, Horror, Romance, Race Relations, or Satire. They were written while the author was in high school and college in the sixties.

Before My Shotgun Wedding is a book for all ages. It is about two best friends growing up in the mountains of Kentucky and going to college before an abusive father with a shotgun forces them to get married.

The sequel, **After My Shotgun Wedding** is for adult readers.

I have eight more novels available for adult readers: **Foundling, Clarence or Claire, Katya and the Solar Wind,** two sequels to **Katya: Triangulation** and **Shoreen; Qarka Girls, Symbiosis, And Angels Feared to Tread** are the most recent science fiction novels to be published.

First Eighty-five Poems was my first volume of poetry. All poems were written between January 1, 1959 and August 1, 1963.

Second Hundred and Sixty-three Poems was my second volume of poetry. All poems were written between August 1963 and March 1967.

Third Hundred and Sixty-eight Poems is my third volume of poetry. These poems were written between March 1967 and March 1981.

Fourth Hundred and Nine Poems is my fourth volume of poetry. They were written between April 7, 1981 and February 23, 2002.

Fifth Volume of Poetry: Falling in Love is my fifth volume of poetry. These poems were written between July 1977 and October 1981.

Sixth Volume of Poetry: Falling in Love Again is my sixth volume of poetry. These poems were written between October 15, 1980 and December 13, 1981.

Seventh Volume of Poetry: Cultivating Love is my seventh volume of poetry. These poems were written between February 1982 and March 1985.

I try to give you a hint of all the feelings I had as I matured as a person. Every one of us has to struggle to be good and kind and loving.

I have loved many girls and women in my life. And a part of me still loves them all. I wish you a lifetime of loving and caring for others and being loved and cared for.

If you are a struggling Christian and have difficulties sorting out your priorities, I had the same kind of problems in my youth. I hope you find my poems meaningful to you. And I suggest that you write your own poetry. Rappers aren't the only people who can express themselves. Everyone can.

As a pastor and theologian, I do not separate the sacred and the profane. The difference is in the human mind and not in life itself, just as evil is in the human mind and comes out of the choices people make and not from the devil who made me do it. The devil has nothing to do with it. We are the ones who choose to do evil or good. The whole world is in our hands.

Enjoy the books.

Paul David Robinson

Paul David Robinson, BA, MDiv, Pastor, Retired

https://www.amazon.com/author/pauldavidrobinson

https://www.pauldavidrobinson.com

www.ingramcontent.com/pod-product-compliance
Lightning Source LLC
Chambersburg PA
CBHW072133170626
46813CB00004BA/1554